Fake Histories

They say today's news is tomorrow's history.
Here are some fake histories that are bound to
come as fake news to someone

৪০০৪

Bob Mynors

Copyright © 2018 Bob Mynors

All rights reserved.

ISBN: **1717110320**
ISBN-13: **978-1717110329**

For my friends and colleagues in
Stannington Library Writers Group,
Ecclesfield Library Writers Group and
Sheffield Central Library Writers
Group, especially group leaders
Sharon Smith and Claire Walker

My thanks to you all for encouraging me, for inspiring me, for giving me confidence, for making me get on with it - and above all for laughing in so very nearly all the right places

CONTENTS

Acknowledgments

IT COMES TOGETHER   1
Fake History of a Taxi Ride

FAKE HISTORIES OF THE PATRON SAINTS OF BRITAIN

A FISHY STORY   9
Fake History of Saint Andrew

MEMORIES: THERE TO BE FORGOTTEN: 15
Fake History of Saint George

THE ACTIONS OF A SIMPLE MAN: 19
Fake History of Saint Patrick
Originally featured in a display of writings on Irish themes in Sheffield Central Library 2018

THE EARTH MOVED: 23
Fake History of Saint David

ALL THIS FUSS   27
Fake History of a Bit of Paper

STRAIGHT FROM THE HORSE'S MOUTH   38
Fake History of a Heist

TO INFINITIVE – AND BEYOND   40
Fake History of the Future

WORLD PEACE AND 'INTERNATIONAL RELATIONS'   51
Fake History of an Artist

CAN'T BUY ME, LOVE 62
Fake History of a Phone Call

THE HAY WAIN 77
Fake History of Art

BYE-BYE, BOBBY DARIN 87
Fake History of a Song

LIVE FROM SANTA'S SLEIGH 97
Fake History of Christmas
Originally featured in Stannington Library Writers Group Christmas Anthology 2015

DISCARDED BY DICKENS 106
Fake History of a Story Never Told

HELTHE & SAFTYE 120
Fake History of Will Shakespeare
Originally featured in 1Stannthology (Stannington Library Writers Group) 2016

VALENTINE'S DAY 145
Fake History of a Hit
Originally featured in Tales from the Library (Ecclesfield Library Writers Group) 2016

DEMON AGREEMENT 156
Fake History of Fake Histories

ACKNOWLEDGMENTS

In this work, I have borrowed fragments of lyric from these songs:
Sailin' (Gavin Maurice Sutherland)
Where Do You Go to, My Lovely? (Peter Sarstedt)
The Fool on the Hill (Paul McCartney, John Lennon)
I Close My Eyes and Count to Ten (Clive Westlake)
Back in the USSR (John Lennon, Paul McCartney)

I have taken *La Mer (Charles Trenet)* and, to the best of my limited ability, rendered it as a song in English

I have taken characters and catchphrases from *Dad's Army (Jimmy Perry, David Croft)* and *Star Trek: the Original Series (Gene Roddenberry, John D F Black, Bob Justman et al)*, using them as if my own by transplanting them into wholly fake situations

In all cases, I have done this with the utmost respect

I have always felt inspired by the original works

Fake Histories is a work of fiction. All the real people, names, places, events and incidents that appear in it are used in ways that are the product of the author's imagination. No claim to truth of any kind in these stories is made, except in the case of facts which are generally attested as part of human history

Running figure on front cover – freepik.com

IT COMES TOGETHER
The Fake History of a Taxi Ride

I had cut it all rather fine. My train was due in at St Pancras at 10.46 and my interview was at 12 o'clock. The taxi ride at the other end should take only about ten or fifteen minutes though so, provided there were no traffic hold-ups, and provided I managed to get a taxi in the first place, I should just about get away with it. I was starting to wish that I'd caught an earlier train, but there was no point worrying about that now. The one before was *The Master Cutler* anyway and I really can't afford those prices

But at least my train set off on time and, as we rattled along, it seemed like it was sticking to the timetable. I had already settled back and opened my *Morning Telegraph*

They're still talking about the moon landing: well - they'll be talking about that for years to come, especially with a bloke on board called Buzz. Mariner 7 has just

1

flown near to Mars. I shall look forward to seeing the pictures from that if there are any. I wonder if they'll be out in time for the Sunday papers: probably not, but maybe next week. Other than that, the news is all a bit depressing - talks in Paris about the war in Viet Nam seem to be going nowhere, all sorts of stuff keeps happening in Northern Ireland and none of it looks good

Oh, here we go, a letter - *what a disgrace it is that Harold Wilson and his Labour Party have allowed yet another piece of our British heritage to be discarded without a thought*. It was only the ha'penny, for goodness sake - and what could you get for a ha'penny these days? Two *Fruit Salads*, two *Black Jacks*? That's all. And that's if they still make *Fruit Salads* and *Black Jacks*, and if they haven't gone up. I bet this bloke hasn't actually spent a ha'penny in years. Yet another act of betrayal by our government to all that is American, the letter-writer calls it. Truth is Americans just wouldn't put up with rubbish like this. They're too intelligent. That President Nixon seems like a much more switched-on sort of bloke. He wouldn't brook any such nonsense

In this way, and with long, long looks through the train window at the speeding countryside, I whiled away the rest of my train journey to London. This was going to be a big day for me. I really wanted the job I was going for, of course, but more than the job I really wanted the interview. I'd lied about my age to be able to get it. And about the work I had done - which was in fact just a Saturday job in a department store, but I'd described it as extensive experience of retail and distribution. I was pretty certain they'd see through me straightaway, but it would be worth it to be able to brag back at home that I had been for a job interview at Lord's Cricket Ground: that would really be something, even if I didn't get to be their new assistant commercial manager

I was up and waiting by the door long before we pulled into the station: longer than I'd intended, if I'm being honest, and I started to feel a bit daft. But I wanted to be the first one off the train, and be down by the taxi rank before anyone else if I could possibly manage it. I'd walked as far down the train as I could to save on distance when I got off, hoping that I'd remembered the layout of St Pancras properly. I was just about sure the front end of the trains pointed to the exit area and that the taxis weren't that far away. I certainly didn't think I was going to have time to take the tube, even if there was a station anywhere near to Lord's, so a taxi was my only option. Probably I should have looked into it all a bit more when I found out I was coming here

I made it to the taxi rank, which was where I thought it was, but no taxis were there, and there was a queue with three people in it. Not for a moment did I suppose that all three would get in one cab together: they didn't. Time was passing by. It was all good news for the taxi drivers, I supposed - no delays in their earnings, but I needed to get a bit of a shift on

It was turning into one of those situations where every minute seems to take half an hour to pass, and everything that happens seems to be working against you. The three people in front of me did all get into separate taxis, and then the gap between the last one of those and mine just went on and on. When finally a fourth one did come into view, it was on the wrong side of the road and had to turn right into the picking up area. But by then, there was an unbroken line of traffic on my side of road and not one of the drivers had got the wit to realise that letting the taxi cross in front of them would take a second and would delay them less. They're all so selfish, these Londoners

It therefore pulled me up a bit when there was a black cab suddenly in front of me. It must have come in on the side of the road near me and I'd just not spotted it. But I got in and barked out my destination. "Lord's Cricket Ground, please."

"Which entrance, mate?"

"Sorry?"

"Which entrance do you want? It'll be on your ticket." The driver was being helpful I now realised. At the same time, I noticed that his voice, though seemingly London, had some deep vestiges of a northern accent lurking in it

"What? Oh - no. I'm not going to watch the cricket. I've got a job interview there. Is there an office entrance?"

"I thought the next match didn't start till tomorrow," he told me, not entirely necessarily, "I can take you to the main gate, and if it's open, I'll take you right up to the door." And we were off

"Where you from then, mate? You sound like you're from up north."

"Yeah I am, and I could say the same about you."

Fake Histories

"You spotted it? Not many do these days. I'm from a place called Stocksbridge. It's in the West Riding. You ever heard of it?"

"Stocksbridge? Sammy Fox's? The Peggy Tub? I know Stocksbridge."

"Ah - the Peggy Tub. It's still there then?"

"Yeah - not that I ever go there. But my Auntie Dolly does. She lives in Stocksbridge."

"I don't think I know your Auntie Dolly."

"You will do. If you're really Stocksbridge, you'll know my auntie Dolly. Everybody does."

Quickly we were in amongst some very leafy, tree-lined streets and big terraced houses, taller than anything I was used to, much posher looking than anything I knew back home. Occasionally there were also blocks of flats, but not like the tower blocks that I've seen going up back in Sheffield. These were probably what people call apartments not flats. Posher again, see

Then, suddenly, we stopped. We pulled in at the side of the road and the driver turned off his engine

"Are we there?" I asked him. I could tell we weren't just by looking round

"We're where we need to be right now," he told me

"We need to be at Lord's Cricket Ground." I was a bit annoyed, but more worried

"Time enough for that mate," he replied. "Just trust me. This is where we need to be right now."

I grabbed the door. My annoyance was catching up with my worry. "I'm getting out," I told the driver

He turned almost fully round and said, "Look mate, I can't tell you anything at the moment, but I really am doing you one of the biggest favours of your life. We need to stop here for about ten or fifteen minutes then I will take you to Lord's and everything will be fine. But you are going to thank me for all of the rest of your life for bringing you here today."

"But …"

"But nothing mate." He really was sounding very insistent now. Part me was worried what on earth he was going to do to me, but other parts were beginning to be intrigued. I knew that Stocksbridge folk, mad though they might be, weren't time-wasters

"But my appointment is important …"

"I know. I know. But, if I'm right, so is this."

"If you're right? You don't even know if it's going to be worth it?"

"I'm sure it is." He was looking me straight in the eyes now. "Look. I had this bloke in the back of the cab last week. He told me that something really special is going to happen right here today, in just a few minutes. And it'll be something that everybody is going to know about and remember for a very long time

"If you get out of the cab now, not only will you probably get lost trying to find your way to Lord's but you'll turn up late even if you don't. If you stay here, I'll get you there in time and we'll both have something to remember forever. Something to tell the grandkids."

Fake Histories

He was right that I would get lost. I didn't even know what direction to set off in. But he was talking nonsense. "So, who was he then, this bloke who's given you this tip off?"

"You promise you'll believe me and you won't laugh?"

"I promise I'll believe you. Whether I laugh or not depends on how daft what you tell me is."

There was a very slight pause, then he said, "Hank Marvin."

I laughed. "Hank Marvin?" I didn't even begin to believe him. "Hank Marvin?" Or did I? "Hank Marvin out of The Shadows?"

"Hank Marvin - out of The Shadows."

"And was Cliff Richard with him? Or was it Billy Fury or Adam Faith or anybody?"

"Look - I had Hank Marvin in the back of my cab last week. He'd been working in that building across the road there. It's a recording studio or something. I do get to bring some of the stars here or pick them up sometimes. And Hank was sitting just there where you are now, and what he told me made me decide that, come what may, I was going to be here right now today. I'm not going to charge you any waiting time or anything ... ooh - look, over there. Something's happening. This is it."

I looked where he was pointing. A group of people had assembled across the road - a pretty odd-looking group at that. There was a bloke with a tall step ladder and he'd got cameras and stuff slung round his neck. There was a copper with them. There were all sorts of other people, and they were all gathering round just at the other side of this zebra crossing. One of them - he did stand out a bit - was wearing a white suit and he'd got long ginger hair and a beard. Another one with long hair and a beard was dressed all in denim. There was a little one in a dark suit with a long jacket like a Mississippi gambler or something. And there was a clean shaven one in a blue suit. He was smoking … and he'd got no shoes on

He'd got no shoes on!

Suddenly it dawned on me. I knew these people. I'd never met them, but I knew all four of them. The whole world knows them - by name. John, George, Ringo and Paul

I don't imagine I need to tell you anymore. Thanks to Stocksbridge - and to Hank Marvin of all people - I was there when one of the world's most famous photographs was taken - the one they used on the front of The Beatles' *Abbey Road* LP

Next time you play the record - and you should play it again, or for the first time if you've never heard it - just look at the cover. Parked up beyond the famous zebra crossing is a black London taxi

FAKE HISTORIES OF THE PATRON SAINTS OF BRITAIN
A FISHY STORY
Fake History of Saint Andrew

Andrew had been involved with the big project from the beginning, along with Simon, his brother, when they all still called him Simon. The two of them had been the first ones invited on to the team, even before James and John. If anything, Andrew had said yes even faster than Simon, though there really wasn't that much in it. But there was no way that Simon - Peter, with all the great works that he had delivered in his great career, was going to own up to anything like that. Andrew's own great works, also now behind him, never seemed quite to measure up to those of his kid brother

Not that the boss ever cared about such things. He had always had his sights set firmly on the task ahead of them, and he made no bones about how tough it was going to be. "Can you hear me," he had asked them at the very outset, "through the dark night far away? I am dying, forever crying to be with you." He was a great one for the metaphor, the boss was: they all thought that. But he could also turn metaphor into literal truth. He had turned out to be absolutely right – like he always was

Back then though, in their naivety, the brothers had smiled at each other, neither thinking it could be any tougher than what they were already doing for a living – they were fishermen, working their boat as a team. They thought this new job offer sounded like swapping a tough life for an all together easier one. And they had turned out to be absolutely wrong – like they so often were. But that was all a long time ago. The original big task was ended now for him, and there was only a bit of consultancy work still on his regular to-do list

This left him with quite a bit of time on his hands. Suddenly he had leisure time, time he could devote to his new hobby which, ironically, was fishing. Not fishing like in the old days, not like when they were out in their little boat on the lake in all but the very worst of weather, hauling heavy nets on board, ripping their hands, straining their joints and doing any amount of damage to their backs. This was fishing for fun, with rod, line and fly. This was calm, intelligent fishing, an intellectual contest between hunter and prey. The list of lands under his influence meant that he had his pick of many of the best lakes and rivers in the world, and this quiet little northern corner offered him some of the best of the best

For some reason, fish had often loomed large in his life. As well as the old job and the new hobby, there had been that other famous occasion, back when the big project had been at its height, when the great convention happened. The boss was going to do one of his speeches, but they had no idea if anyone would be there to listen. They'd all put the word out round the local towns, inviting everybody they came across, and then just hoped somebody would turn up. In the end, they need not have worried. It seemed like pretty much everybody had come to see what was going on – everybody, that is, except for a catering crew. That was the kind of oversight that happened sometimes, but this time it looked as though it might blow the whole show out of the water. For once even the boss looked at a loss, like even he needed someone to dig him out of the situation

That was the moment when the youngster showed up - looking a bit sheepish, looking quite frankly scared. It was easy to see why. He was there on his own it seemed, in amongst a huge crowd and all of them were calling for food, expecting it to rain down from the sky or make some other miraculous appearance. And he was just a young lad with a packed lunch his mother or someone must have made for him, worried to death that someone was going to snatch it from him - or worse. "I'm going to have to do something here," Andrew thought. "I'd better take the kid to the boss before anything happens to him. The boss will know what to do."

The look on the boss's face when Andrew and the boy stood before him was a picture, something no one who ever saw it will forget. It had been a look of worry moments earlier, and the transformation was like – there was no other word for it – like a miracle. Finally, the boss had something he could work with. It took only a moment to persuade the lad to hand his lunch over. There was little enough of it, but the way the boss used it was completely outside the box

With what seemed little more than a click of his fingers – though it surely must have been more than that – he had everyone's attention again, the whole crowd. He held up the boy for everyone to see, introduced him, showed him to the crowd, then announced the generosity of this young boy who was standing with them wanting to share his lunch with everyone. People started forming up in lines, without even the merest pause. He could certainly work a crowd, the boss

As food was handed to them, it seemed all the people assembled suddenly found odd bits of food about them so they wanted to make donations too. Everybody took from the pile of food, and at the same time everybody gave. It was a sight to behold. It could hardly have been slicker (or more obvious to anyone who thought about it even for a second or three) if it had been a routine in a Marx Brothers movie. But it has gone down in the books as one of the great miracles

Some say this was when the ploy of using the fish symbol to represent the boss and his works started – especially useful during all the persecutions that were to follow. But Andrew wasn't sure. He didn't like the other main theory either – that the first letter of the boss's name in Greek (Χριστός) – looks a bit like a fish. He thought it looked no more like a fish than it did a camel – or a flying eagle or any number of other things. But he would not have got into a fight over it

Back at the convention, when it was all over, and when there was still plenty of food to collect and redistribute elsewhere, at first Andrew just looked on and watched the others doing some of the work for a change. But suddenly he couldn't resist the temptation to pick up his staff, take a firm two-handed grip on it, move alongside one of the left-over loaves, address it, give it a firm but gentle tap with the end of the staff and knock it neatly into a nearby hole. "In one!" he thought to himself, mentally punching the air

Of course, fishy things are not always good things: sometimes fish stinks. The reason he had ended up taking on responsibility for this little northern corner of the world had always struck him as spurious. The folk who lived there, with their red hair and painted faces, were staring at an invasion from the stronger and much more numerous people from the south. The odds were not good, but the local leader called upon the sky for a sign. The sky replied with a saltire - long, wispy white clouds crossed against the otherwise clear blue canopy. Or so it was alleged. "I am flying," the leader is supposed to have cried out, "passing high clouds to be with you, to be free."

"Some people will believe anything," is what Andrew thought.. But the blue and white saltire had always been his symbol, and the fishing was good here, so he didn't mind

And that is how, in a series of unlikely events, the nation of Scotland got its patron saint, its flag, its national game and one of its more popular tourists pursuits, and how one of its best known ex-pats got one of his greatest hit songs – even though it took a different one to write it

MEMORIES: THERE TO BE FORGOTTEN
Fake History of Saint George

"Where do you go to, my lovely?" How often had his wife brought him back to the world with such gentle words? He knew it must worry her that he could become so deeply lost in reverie as he tried to recall all that had happened in his long life

So much of it was consigned now to memory - all that had happened to bring the two of them together the way they were today. There was so much to remember, which also meant there was so much to forget. He did forget much. He knew he did. And he knew he could never hope to remember what it was. And that irked him

He remembered he had been born a Greek and had lived a Roman, first with his father and mother in Anatolia, later with only his mother in Syria Palestina. But so much of his life seemed as if it were lost in a mist, a mist that came with age or else with distance - he was less than sure which

At times he fancied he had earlier been a soldier, a fighter, a leader amongst men: he knew that many called on him now to support or give blessing to their causes in conflict. But again he fancied he had been previously a priest, a bishop even. Had he not freed slaves? Had he not distributed wealth and lands among the people? He thought he had

Sometimes it was hard even to remember his own name. He had so many, it seemed, in so many places. He had names he had never heard in in lands he had never set foot on. And he had a duty of care for places of which he knew little or nothing. Just as an instance, there was that funny one they had given him to watch out for, the one that was most but not all of an island in the far northern sea, but they had also given him most of the rest of Europe as well, and large chunks of the rest of the world. This meant he often had both sides praying to him for intercession. It was all a bit much, especially for one whose memory was receding so fast

There were all the little places too, the cities and towns whose names meant nothing to him, all calling on him for succour and inspiration. "It must be a good thing," he thought. "It must be a mark of something to be so loved and so trusted by so many people. If only I could remember why ... If only I could remember ..."

He remembered his wife. He remembered how much he loved her: he remembered how much she loved him. Dear ... dear ... he would remember her name in a moment. It mattered little though, alongside their love which mattered so much more. He remembered her father too ... no, his name was also gone, but he remembered still what that man had almost done to his daughter. There was no forgetting that, or forgiving such cruelty

And now he seemed to be responsible personally for so many people, and for so many things, which was hard. Always there seemed to be sheep and their shepherds about the place, all seeking his approval. And who were all these boys? These young men? There was a time when they appeared to be almost everywhere with their silly hats and their long sticks and their constant marching to and fro, lighting fires and making tea and tying knots and singing round campfires. Not quite so many now. And what had all those bright yellow flashes they used to insist people put in their windows? What had they been about? And had he been responsible for them? Had he been responsible for putting a stop to them?

Then there were the days when it felt like a hospital out there, like a bad day in a badly run doctor's surgery. People called on him for care and for assistance for all manner of things. People turned up with their nasty ailments like herpes or leprosy or syphilis: how had he come to be shouldering that particular load, as well as intervening on behalf of all the farm workers and all the saddle makers and all the soldiers - and all the rest of them?

Better just to relax and think of his wife, and of the day they met, the day he rescued her from — whatever it was. A monster breathing fire, flapping its leathern wings? An overbearing man with bad breath, odd-coloured hair and an unforgiveable attitude to women? "Whatever sort of monster it was, my love, I would fight it again for you today if I needed to. If you asked me to." He looked for his wife but didn't see her, and he whispered, "Where did you go to, my lovely?"

And that is how, gradually but inexorably, the nation of England gained its patron saint, but was forced to share with Portugal and Canada and Ethiopia and Montenegro and Palestine and Georgia and all the rest, how everyone from a member of the Order of the Garter to any scruffy little oik with a skin rash gained someone to turn to in times of need, and how the inspiration was laid for a son of the British Raj to write and perform a folky and romantic sort of waltz about the decadence of the European jet-set in the 20th Century

THE ACTIONS OF A SIMPLE MAN:
the Fake History of Saint Patrick

Day after day, alone on a hill, the man with the foolish grin was sitting perfectly still. "Well you would do, wouldn't you?" Patrick might have observed to any passer-by querying his position. "You would want to conserve your energy in a situation like this." But no one did pass by, and he remained completely quiet

He was just a simple man and was wondering why, when the Lord had spoken unto him, a forty-day fast had been such an important requirement. It was very far from clear, but you didn't argue with the orders – not if you wanted to continue the forward career momentum

He'd served his time, mostly in Autissiodorum (in the modern world called Auxerre) and Turones (now Tours), and was looking to capitalise on this by achieving high office. His only disappointment was that it looked like it was going to have to be high office here in Hibernia, right out on the edge of the Empire. It wasn't even as if he'd been born here or anything. It seemed a bit unfair

At least though he had chosen a sensible spot for his fast, under a bit of an overhang that kept much of the rain off, and with a little spring nearby so he could slake his thirst and not go completely potty. There was also a scrubby little bush there that gave him some shelter from the wind – some. And he had to admit that, every once in a while, he had picked a few of the berries from the bush and eaten them. It didn't feel really like breaking his fast, they were so small, but it eased the worst of the hunger The berries weren't even very nice, he thought. In fact, they were awful. Nobody would willingly want to use these for human consumption but "needs must," he thought. He tried to remember what the bush was called, and it came back to him. "Iuniperorum - juniper." He leaned back on the cold stone of the hillside, contemplating another dreary day there. "The fast days go so slow," he thought, and smiled – a thin, worried smile. "Maybe I should take more of that water with it."

Suddenly there was a movement on the ground. His eyes darted towards the movement as he pulled back his foot, though not before his foot felt a sharp pain. "It's a snake!" he yelled. "A bloody snake. It just bit me." As he looked about, he saw there was not just one but dozens of the slithering little creatures. No, hundreds. "That does it," he bellowed, and he stood up. His foot actually only hurt a bit

Picking up his staff, he beat the ground with it. As he did so, the snakes turned tail, if that's not an oxymoron, hurrying away from him. And he chased after them, beating his staff on the ground all the while and yelling. And the more he beat down with his staff and the more he yelled, the more snakes there were fleeing from him

He chased them down the hill and across the plain until they finally reached a cliff overlooking the sea. Here he did suffer momentary doubts. He really wasn't sure what would happen next, but he needn't have worried. The host of snakes now assembled just kept going – all of them – right over the cliff

He stopped at the cliff's edge and looked down. It wasn't a very high cliff, and the snakes all seemed to survive the drop and just kept on slithering out into the sea. No – not slithering any more. He noticed, as the last few snakes landed on the pebble beach below, that they all – every last one of the blighters – seemed to have sprouted tiny legs and feet - tiny little legs and feet that were working overtime. The snakes were all scurrying now into the sea

But he'd watched enough. He wanted to get back to his hill and his fast. He realised he had done exactly what he knew he should not have done – wasted a lot of energy. He wanted to go and rest. And he did. He settled down under his overhang. He drank more than a little of his water. He sneaked a few more of his juniper berries. And a few more. He leaned back, tired, and saw the sun going down. And he drifted off to sleep, but the eyes in his head still saw the world spinning round

What he didn't see was the sight of all the snakes he had chased from his island swimming across the sea and, with their tiny legs and feet, climbing out on to the island next door, at a point some way to the south where the current had carried them all

And that is how, on a single day, and using modern parlance, the actions of a simple man led to the island of Ireland being rid of all its snakes, to the same island gaining its patron saint, to the Lizard Point in what would later be called England gaining its name, to gin being almost invented, though not quite, and to the inspiration being laid for one of the most sentimental songs created by the 20th Century pop group, The Beatles

THE EARTH MOVED:
the Fake History of Saint David

It had not been there before. David at least had no memory of it having been there before. He closed his eyes and counted to ten, and when he opened them, it was still there

"It's a funny thing," he said to no one in particular, "but if you had asked me if they had come up a hill to get here, I would have laughed and said, 'You what? Of course they didn't. What hill?' Yet there they all are – undeniably, irrefutably – walking back down a hill they never walked up in the first place, and all singing their heads off as they go."

The crowd seemed oblivious to all such thoughts. All had been uplifted by the words he had delivered. All strode amiably away now, down the gentle slope as if it were the most natural thing in the world. It must say something about the quality of the performance he had just given them – not one that raised the roof, maybe, but one that raised the floor

David smiled, and a white dove fluttered down and settled on his shoulder. "How many of my fellows can make a claim like this?" he thought to himself. "It must be time to step up a gear and move the act on to the next level."

Yet on the following day, he was disappointed to hear reports that his detractors – of which he had many - were dismissing the incident. One went so far as to claim it would be difficult to *conceive of any miracle more superfluous* than the creation of a new hill in this landscape already replete with them. Oh, he would make them eat their words one day – one day: for every new hill, there is, after all, a new valley. And his people loved their valleys, and sang about them to anyone would listen

Now though a different, more important and more urgent task lay before him. The nation was under attack. His holy office prevented him from picking up a weapon himself, but his heart ruled his head, "*Ar gyfer hen wlad fy nhadau*," he thought. "For the old land of my fathers." He felt compelled to play some part. When he reached the field of battle, a near hopeless sight greeted him. Defender and invader were indistinguishable. All were caked in mud and blood, and weapons fell as often upon friend as upon foe. But it was the invaders who had strength in reserve: they might well prevail through sheer weight of numbers. The thought brought tears to David's eyes and pain to his heart

As he sniffed to conceal the weakling emotions he was experiencing, something unexpected happened to him. Amongst the stench of blood and mud and battle, he could smell something else – something like an onion. Not an onion. Something like a leek. Looking round, he spied a field of the aromatic plant. This gave him an idea

He grabbed two boys from the back of the defending force, boys too young even to be there at all let alone try to fight an invader. He dragged them with him towards the field. They almost escaped him when their countrymen began to jeer them for cowards, thinking they were running from the battle. But he harried the boys and took them with him into the field where he had them help him gather armfuls of the leeks. These they carried back to the battlefield, where, without fuss, he and the boys began thrusting the vegetables into the belts of the tunics worn by their countrymen. The green and white of the leeks shone out against the blood red that besmeared so many battle tunics. Every fighter was told to look for the leek, to strike only those not wearing them

Fighters at the front of course did not yet know this. Nor had anyone yet given them a leek to wear. But brave men fought through from the rear, distributing both the story and the leeks as they slashed and bludgeoned their way past blood soaked bodies, relying heavily on noting which way each fighting man was facing to guess which side he might be on. Slowly, and despite many setbacks, the leeks held the day: the invaders were repelled.

Victory was celebrated with leeks held high as tunics dripped yet with foreign blood

News of this victory and all that led to it spread far and fast. Invitations rolled in from all corners for David to visit, to repeat his words and actions in many parts. Practically, there were few he could fulfil, but one he did was at the fabled town of Glastonbury. Again he took to a dais in a wide open space before a throng. He used the words he had used before. Again the ground moved – but this time it did not rise: it simply slid away as the heavens opened and rain fell and fell upon all. He took in the sight. He closed his eyes and counted to ten, and when he opened them, it was all still there. And the people loved it. And they cheered him, and they chanted his name, and they danced and cavorted in the mud

And that is how, in succession so quick the modern mind can barely credit it, the nation of Wales gained its patron saint, and its national symbol, and its national anthem, and the colour of its national rugby jersey, whilst Glastonbury became almost magically associated with rain and revelry, and the inspiration was laid for a young Welshman called Clive to write one of the greatest hits of 20th Century singer Dusty Springfield

ALL THIS FUSS
Fake History of a Bit of Paper

"But I gave it to you," he told me, sharply. I was always getting blamed for things, but I know I'd given him his precious bit of paper back. He'd just forgotten it and wasn't going to own up, that's all. I'd get told off if I tried that

I didn't like how the governor was starting to sound - even bossier than usual. And it seemed like there was nothing else I could do. I was in big trouble, and there was nowhere to go and hide, nowhere at all, in this cramped little space. Tempers weren't half getting frayed

"You did give it to me, sir. But I know I gave it back to you. I will look again, I suppose, but I don't see why ..."

"Stop mumbling, boy, and just do as you're told."

It might just have slipped down to the bottom of one of the boxes, I supposed. I just wish he wouldn't keep going on at me. It really wasn't fair. My mum says I shouldn't let people push me around so much at work, but it isn't easy - not the way he goes off

"Well get on with it," the governor ordered, adding under his breath, like he nearly always does, "Stupid boy!" But I'm not stupid and I wish he wouldn't keep on saying I am. He can get quite pompous sometimes, the governor. Anyway, I was still sure he hadn't given the blinkin' thing back me. And it was only a bit of paper with some words scribbled on it after all, so why did it matter so much? We all knew what it said. But if I hadn't got it, then either he'd given it to someone else or, which was much more likely to be the case, he'd still got it himself somewhere

"I don't see why it's all that important," I grumbled. "It's only a bit of paper." I could feel myself starting to snivel a little bit, and I wished again that there was somewhere I could go and get out of his way so he wouldn't see me. But there wasn't

"Don't see why it's all that important?" Now he put on that voice of his, the one he always uses when he thinks he has to explain things as if the rest of us are all idiots and he's the only one who ever knows anything. "That *bit of paper* as you call it is the whole point of this business. I have to show that bit of paper to some very important people so they can see that we have done what we set out to do. If I turn up and tell them that it was *only a bit of paper* and we *didn't think it was all that important*, I'm sure they would give me very short shrift. And I for one wouldn't blame them."

I could feel my bottom lip starting to go now and I certainly didn't want him to see that, so I buried my head in my box to look like I was still searching for it, and just hoped it would all go away

By now, I think everybody else was starting to feel a bit embarrassed. Some of them obviously thought they could help the situation by chipping in their usual contributions. I could probably have told you what they were all going to say before any of them had even opened their mouths

"Don't panic!" That was Jack, of course. "Don't panic!" He always said that and it just made him panic even more than he already was doing

It would James next, I thought, muttering half under his breath in his heavy Scots accent. I was right: he muttered, "Doomed. We're all doomed." And he rolled his eyes as he said it. I'm sure he thought saying it so softly would allow him to claim credit for predicting it if the whole thing ended in disaster, but that he could deny saying anything at all if we somehow managed to get away with it

I looked across at Arthur. He was the only one in the bunch who was really nice to me, and he seemed always to have my interests at heart. Sometimes I think I looked on him like a kind of uncle. Just like I thought he would, he made the next contribution. "Would you chaps mind awfully not ribbing Frank just now? It's hardly helping the situation."

I felt a warm wave of relief and gratitude flow over me, knowing one person at least was on my side despite all the grumbling from the others. "Thank you, Arthur," I told him. I wanted him to put his arm round my shoulder like he sometimes had done before - but he didn't

Instead, he said, "Now we must find this elusive piece of paper, Frank. It really is jolly important after all. Are you sure you've looked in all your pockets?"

His voice was gentle and soothing. "Yes, Arthur," I told him

"Would you like me to check for you?"

"Oh, stop mollycoddling the boy, Arthur." This was the governor again. "He'll never develop any sense of responsibility if you keep on talking to him as if he's still in the nursery. We need some positive action if we're going to find this thing. Just take off your jacket and trousers, boy, and I'll search through your pockets."

"What?" I heard myself call out. "I'm not taking my trousers off in front of everybody."

"Oh, stop making such a fuss." Sometimes the governor treated me like I was still at school - and it just wasn't fair. "You haven't got anything we've not all seen before."

"You've not got anything we haven't all seen before either," I told him, "but I don't suppose you'll be taking your trousers off to let me search through your pockets."

"Don't you take that tone of voice with me, boy."

"Permission to speak, sir." Jack had served in the trenches during the war, and in the Sudan or so he always told us, so he always treated the governor like a commanding officer. "I should like to volunteer to take young Frank's jacket and trousers off, sir, and search through his pockets."

"Oh, settle down, Jack. I don't think that will be necessary," the governor told him. Under his breath, to Arthur, he whispered, "I'm beginning to worry a little bit about Jack."

"Really, sir?"

"Yes – er - his enthusiasm can be just a little – well - overwhelming sometimes."

"I know what you mean, sir."

No one else heard what they were saying: they were all too busy searching again through the boxes they had already searched through before. But I heard it

All was silent for a moment, until Charles, who had not said anything yet, decided to say his piece. "My sister says we all waste far too much time looking for things when all that ever happens is that we find the last thing we were looking for."

We all stared at him. The governor pinched the top of his nose, flattened his moustache with his forefinger and his thumb, then he said, "I'm sure we all thank you, and your sister of course, for sharing that with us Charles, but I'm afraid I fail to see how it helps."

"Well sir, I think what my sister would say is that we shouldn't just keep on looking for this thing. I think she'd advise us to stop looking for it and look for something else instead. Then we'd be sure to find the last thing we were looking for - which is the thing we were all looking for in the first place."

After another silence, the governor piped up again. "Come on, Frank. We haven't got all day. We've got to get this piece of paper found and we are running out of time. Get those bags off."

"But sir …," and I couldn't think of anything else to say at this point so I was very relieved when Joe became the last one in the party to speak

"Hold on, guv'nor. I've just had an idea. It will get us all off the hook and it will save young Frankie-boy here from showing us a side of his character that none of us really wants to see."

"I hope this will be a sensible suggestion, Joe. We've all suffered more than enough of your red herrings over the years."

"No. Straight up, guv'nor. This is a proper idea. Nothing dodgy. Nothing under the counter, so to speak. I just need to ask you a couple questions to see if it's an idea that will sink or swim."

The governor heaved a very resigned sigh and said, "Very well. Go on then. I don't suppose we have much to lose at this point. Just don't try to involve me in any of the disreputable shenanigans you usually bring us, and please don't try to waste my time or I shall have some very harsh things to say to you afterwards. And you will regret hearing them."

"Guv'nor. You wound me. When have I ever let you down? No - don't answer that, but you'll agree I have saved us from a terrible fate more than once, haven't I?"

The governor hummed and harred a little, but Joe was sounding quite full of himself by this point. I was sure he wouldn't let us down, especially me, and couldn't wait to hear his idea

"Right. First tell me this. When we find this perishin' bit o'paper and you take it to show to these important people of yours - they are going to be important, aren't they?"

"Oh yes - yes. Very important," the governor confirmed. "Very important indeed."

"Well when you show it to them, how closely are they going to look at it?"

"Very closely indeed, I should imagine."

"What - all of 'em?"

"We-ell. Not the first few, I don't suppose. For them, I imagine I shall merely have to hold it up. Most of them will be looking at it from some distance."

"And when you've done that, you're going to take it away for these nobs, these VIPs, to give it the old once over?"

"Ye-es. I suppose that is one way of putting it."

"Well. There you are then. There's your answer."

James' dry Scots voice made itself heard again. "Yon Sassenach is so used to spinning his yarns to others, he thinks we'll all fall for them."

But Jack interrupted him. "No - hold on Jock. I think Joe might be on to something. Keep talking, Joe."

"Well - don't you see, sir? That gives us just the time we need."

"I trust you're not going to suggest any kind of subterfuge, Joe: no sleight of hand or anything."

I could feel the need to take my trousers off in front of everybody fading away, but I decided to keep quiet, just so as not to remind anybody I was there

Joe continued. "I'm just trying to buy us some time, guv'nor, and without us having to pay for it, if you see what I mean. We all know it's in here, don't we, the piece of paper? We all saw it in here. We all know it must still be in here somewhere. We just need a bit more time to look for it and make sure that we find it. If you go out there and show them something they think is the real McCoy, they'll all be happy. Then the rest of us can stay in here and find the proper one so you can take it with you and hand it to the people who really matter."

"I think I can see what Joe is getting at." Arthur caught on much faster than the governor. "You will only need to have in your hand a piece of paper, any old piece of paper, for the first people you see because they won't have a chance or a need to examine it."

"But the gentlemen of the press will be out there, photographers, the BBC, possibly even the newsreels."

I'm afraid I did get a bit over-excited at the mention of newsreels. I jumped up and shouted, "Ooh! Pathé News. Cock-a-doodle-doo!"

Arthur looked at me very sternly. "Frank. Will you please calm down? You're still supposed to be looking for it, remember. Just get on with doing that."

But he couldn't stop me hearing another whispered *stupid boy* from the governor, who then added, "I'm sure there won't be any of that French nonsense there anyway. I imagine I shall be addressing British Movietone News."

When Arthur asked him if British Movietone wasn't owned by the Americans, he said, "That is just the kind of cynical remark I would expect from an Eton boy. At Rugby, we always believed patriotism was a virtue." I think he was trying to put Arthur in his place. But then, with a sudden change in his tone, he went on, "But I think I do see some value in Joe's suggestion. After all, one of our responsibilities is keeping up the people's morale. But I have no wish to be seen as anything other than completely honest about this affair. So much depends on it. So much. Where is my speech, Arthur?"

"Here it is, sir."

The governor took the sheet of paper Arthur held out to him, and inspected it very closely. Then he reached out his free hand, still looking at the paper, and said, "Pen, please, Arthur."

"I'm afraid I don't have a pen with me, sir."

Now the governor looked at him, most sternly

"Why on Earth have you come on a mission of this importance and not brought a pen with you? Sometimes, Arthur, you are completely irresponsible."

"I've a pencil you can borrow if that will help." Arthur's attempt at being helpful didn't work

"No, a pencil won't help. It won't help at all. I can't make notes on a document of this importance with a pencil. Do have some sense of proportion."

"But it's not an important document, is it, sir? It's only your speech."

Arthur was really taking chances now. After mumbling something that sounded like *dashed impertinence*, the governor snapped at him. "Someone of your seniority should always have a pen at the ready – for any circumstance. You ought to know that."

"Well I did have one when we set out, sir," Arthur sounded almost bored as he said it, "but the person who borrowed it from me has yet to give it back."

The governor grunted as he took a pen from his pocket, a pen that looked exactly one of Arthur's, and made what seemed a very few changes with it to the words written on the paper. He returned the pen to his pocket, then stood up and said to me, "Pass me my overcoat, boy. I'm going out there."

"Before you do sir," Charles had shuffled to the front, "I wonder if I might be excused …"

"Certainly not, Charles," the governor snapped. "There's no time and besides, there's nowhere in here to excuse you to."

As I handed his coat to him, something fell from the folds – a piece of paper by the look of it. But before I could bend down to pick it up, Arthur placed his foot over it. Almost imperceptibly he shook his head at me

I think someone - probably James but I don't know - mumbled something like, "The old fool'll never get away with it." I couldn't swear it was him though

I helped the governor put his coat on and, after he had fastened just one button and brushed down his lapels with his hands, he lowered his head and set off through the door of the Lockheed 14, out on to the grass of Heston Aerodrome

Fake Histories

Applause began immediately. We could all hear it inside the plane. But it fell silent as soon as the governor started to speak. There were the usual pleasantries at the start, but soon he was into the real meat of the speech. "This morning I had another talk with the German Chancellor, Herr Hitler, and here is the paper which bears his name upon it as well as mine. Some of you, perhaps, have already heard what it contains but I would just like to read it to you."

We didn't wait to hear any more though. We were busy shaking hands and congratulating each other. Mr Chamberlain had done it. He'd saved the day. Even miserable old James was forced to admit that he had never doubted for a minute that he would bring peace for our time

STRAIGHT FROM THE HORSE'S MOUTH
Fake History of a Heist

I don't like being woken up suddenly - but the place is full of noise and movement. There are people everywhere and they're all shouting, shouting, shouting

Can't a horse get a decent night's kip in here?

I've got a big race coming up the week after next and I'm supposed to be in training, and they're going off like this

Give us a break, will you?

I'd have a word with that Michael Stoute if I thought he knew anything about horses, or even cared about us. But he doesn't. He just manages to surround himself with people who make us work hard for him and make him look good

Hang on a minute though. Some of these people are not stable lads. Not unless they've just come back from a fancy-dress party or something. They're coppers, aren't they? The place is crawling with police – real ones

Why doesn't somebody tell me what's going on? I'm a horse, not an idiot

Oh, I get it. It'll be his lordship again. Everything has to revolve around him - just because he's won a few more races than the rest of us, and everybody goes all weak at the knees when he gets on the telly

But he gets all the best treatment, all the best fodder, all the best jockeys. We could all be superstars if we got treatment like that. So where is the old nag? What's he been up to this time? Thrown a shoe, has he? Tripped over his own hooves? You'd think the sun shone out from under his tail

Hang on a minute though: Stoutey's here. Must be something bloody important to drag him out of his bed at this time of night

Oh my God! Somebody's stolen him. Somebody's stolen Shergar

Well - good. Maybe the rest of us will get a bit more respect now

I hope he ends up in a can!

TO INFINITIVE – AND BEYOND
Fake History of the Future

I don't know. I really thought winning the contract to create the public information video for one of the biggest projects ever undertaken by anyone anywhere in the entire history of communication would be some kind of a feather in my cap. At the very least. And a way of stepping up to other, bigger projects. What I did not know in advance was that I would be working with the biggest crew of interfering cheapskates it has ever been my misfortune to rub up against. The re-writes - the refused access to official material - the pared-down production facilities - I had to put up with all of these

It will be a wonder if anyone anywhere takes any notice at all of this thing. Yet they still want me to deliver the biggest thing since Jaws first ate sliced bread with a cat playing the piano in the background. But just look at this place, will you? The cheapest street-corner pay-by-the-hour recording studio in town. And they're paying direct. In fact, they've pre-paid, which means when the time runs out, everything will just shut down. The screens will go black, the sound systems will click off and even the lights will go out. I'll only be able to get out of here by the light coming through the little observation window in the door

But enough with the whingeing already. There's not much time, so we'd better get on

"OK everybody. We're going for a take. Everybody quiet. Tape rolling. Mike on. Recording in three - two - one …"

"Space: the final frontier. These are the voyages of the Starship Enterprise. Its five-year mission: to explore strange new worlds, to seek out new life and new civilizations, to boldly go where no …"

"Cut! Cut! Cut!" He had done it again. "Look, Jim, baby, we gotta get this right and we're running out of time." Can you believe it? He had done it again, after all the times we'd talked it through. "This is the mission statement. This is your mission statement. This is the statement defines your mission, that your whole mission depends on. You don't want all the cynical grammar snowflakes out there to be laughing behind your back for the next few centuries, do you?

"You've got the script there in front of you. It's the script that Star Fleet have all seen, the one that the United Federation of Planets have all seen. It's the one that all the media corporations across the whole of the Alpha Quadrant have seen. Everybody who gives even the slightest shit for what your mission is about already knows what's in it

"And when we post this video and invite the world - the galaxy - to look at it, if you say something different, something that's not there on the page, they will just drop on us, on you and on me: they will drop on us like a ton of Klingon battle debris."

I knew what he was going to tell me. It would be the same thing he had told me about a dozen times already - every time we'd gone for a read-through. Every take we'd gone for. It's the reason why we'd had to leave the mission statement right to the very end of the schedule - to give the Canadian klutz the time he needed to take the words on board. And he just wasn't playing ball

"But I'm just reading what it says on the sheet here in front of me."

I had had this conversation too many times. "No you aren't, Jim. You're reading what you think it says." I had started to become very frustrated with this highly paid bus driver. OK - unfair I know. There is definitely more to captaining a starship than there is to driving a bus

"You're reading what you want it to say, what you're just hoping to hell it does say, because for some reason your brain - your brain that is big enough and smart enough to command the most important and expensive vessel that Star Fleet has ever built and launched - that brain is refusing to see ten little characters in plain black and white on the sheet of paper that's on the desk in front of you. Come on, Jim. Come on. It's there in front of you for Chrissakes! Jim - work with me, please. Concentrate, and read the words that have been written for you."

Everyone I'd ever spoken to about this man told me he was renowned throughout Star Fleet for his sense of fair play, his insistence that no one should ever suffer just because of low status in an organisation. I was hoping I could invoke this by appealing from my own status that was very low, and falling fast

"It's the split infinitive thing that's bugging you, isn't it Morey?"

"Yes, Jim. It's the split infinitive thing - and we have talked about it many times. And I know what you think about it, but you know what your options are." Not again, Jim. Please – not - again. I saw the minutes ticking away on the control room clock

"Well it's not helping that I have two different versions here in front of me. If you're giving me choices, why does the one I want to choose not make it on to the list?"

I turned to Rose-Marie, my assistant on the project, and asked her if she would mind just running round to the booth where Jim was sitting and make sure he only had one version of the script in front of him - the correct version

"Jim. You know I respect you enormously, don't you? You know I was already involved in the mission even before you were selected from the list of candidates to head it. You know all of that because you saw me making the video record during all the tests and trials that you and the other Star Fleet people went through

"Now I'm not trying to compare my tiny role in the success of the mission to your huge and absolutely pivotal one. But please don't think that makes me any less committed to its success than you are, because that would simply not be true."

"Calm down, Morey. I know you're a good man, and I'm happy to be working with you."

"Tell me then, do you remember sitting in that bar with me, back on the lunar base two years ago, the night before they chose the mission commander?"

"Yes, Morey. I remember it very well. You helped me through a difficult time. I was nervous, more nervous than I have been since I was teenager first trying to persuade the girl students at the Academy to - drop their inhibitions. And you told me that if Star Fleet didn't name me as mission commander, then everyone else on the mission might as well resign straight away because that would mean it was being put together by idiots."

"Thank you for remembering that. And I wasn't shooting you no line back then, Jim. I sure wasn't being nice to you because you'd just bought me a synth-ale. I knew you were the man for the job. I knew then like I know now that when you take this mission out beyond the Alpha, beyond known space, that you will stand up to those alien freaks like a man and show them that the Federation way is the right way, the only way."

"Alien freaks?"

"You know what I mean."

"So what does all this have to do with my mission statement?"

"What all this has to do with your mission statement - which is our mission statement, by the way, Jim - is that just as I respect you as a starship commander, then I wish you would respect me as a communicator, as a movie maker. I have my mission too, you know - to create new movies, to present new messages and new images, to make all the goddam morons out there in Federation space believe in your mission because if they start to have doubts about it and the politicians get cold feet, then we're screwed. All of us. You, me, your crew, your ground support team, the whole mission command structure. And I don't want to see that happen,"

Of course, he came straight back at me. "So how does - what did you say it was? Ten little characters in black and white on a sheet of paper? How can they keep these morons as you call them on side? Especially when they don't even get to see the paper. They just hear me say the words."

"It's all in the message, Jim. It's having the right message, saying the right message, saying it every time, and only saying it - not deviating from it. You're deviating from it right at the start

"Now Rose - you know Rose-Marie, don't you? - Rose is on her way to you now to make sure you have just the one version of the mission statement in front of you. The proper one. The version we need to hear. We've got the version you keep reading on tape more times than I care to think about: you haven't given me the right one once yet. Please, Jim. Can we just do it the way it's been written? Just once? Just to humour me? We'll probably only have time for one last take anyway the way time is running out on us."

"Well I was reading up on this whole split infinitive thing the other day, Morey, and what I read said that the Smithsonian Institute no less put the whole thing to bed back in the 21st Century. They said that split infinitives just don't matter anymore. In fact, they said that split infinitives don't even exist - that there's nothing there even to split."

"Smithsonian Institute, eh?"

"That's right. Not just anybody, Morey, but the actual Smithsonian Institute."

Another voice intervened. "Morey? Morey? Can I have a word?"

"'Scuse me a moment, Jim. Rose-Marie is trying to talk to me. Yes Rose. Have you got to Jim yet?"

"I shall be in the booth with him in a moment, but you also asked me to give you the word when you're down to five minutes of studio time."

"Five minutes? Already?"

"Well, you've actually got six, but I need to go out and get lunch when I've sorted out the captain so I thought I'd let you know now."

"OK. Thanks Rose. And can you get me a corned beef sandwich with mustard whilst you're out there. And a piece of fruit. Get me a nice piece of fruit."

"Will do, Morey. And will the captain want anything?"

"Jim — Rose-Marie wants to know if you need her to pick up anything for you for lunch. We get good sandwiches here. Made with real ingredients."

"No. That's kind of her, Morey. Thank her for me, but I'll eat when I get back to the base. I find I prefer replicator food these days."

"He says he's OK, Rose, but he thanks you for thinking of him. He also says he prefers his food replicated, if you can believe that."

"That's a very sad thing to hear, Morey. I hope he doesn't take all his pleasures from replicators. And you've got four minutes now. See you later."

"OK Jim. She'll be with you in just a few moments. She's one cute kid, Jim. I certainly don't think it would take you long to get her to - what did you call it? - drop her inhibitions."

"Morey!"

"And I don't know if you heard what she said, Jim, but we've got about four minutes of studio time left, maybe only three now, so there's no leeway. The time ends and the systems shut down immediately. You won't be able to hear me and I won't be able to hear you. The lights will go out, the doors will fly open and we shall be outside.

And if we haven't got the whole thing in the can by then, there'll be a couple admirals I can think of who are gonna be after my ass. And I'm afraid I shall have to hand them yours too."

"But the Smithsonian …"

"Will you forget about the Smithsonian Institute, Jim? Even the eggheads at the Smithsonian don't know everything. They don't get it right every time."

"Don't they?"

"Of course they don't. They backed down over that Enola Gay thing, didn't they?"

"Enola Gay thing? When was that?"

"I don't know. Back in the 20th Century, I suppose, or the 21st. When it was pointed out to them that dropping an atomic bomb on an enemy state we were at war with wasn't automatically an act of cowardice or treason, then they backed down."

"So who was doing the pointing out? The CIA? Fox News? Wikileaks?"

"OK. OK. So I don't know if the story's true. It could have been made up by some kid with a Twitter account and a heightened sense of destiny or just a warped sense of humour for all I care. But it doesn't matter. What matters is that we record your speech - properly - and get both of us out of here before the meter clicks on to zero. Look - I'm gonna talk you very quickly through the two options. You'll have to decide there and then which one you're gonna go with. Rose-Marie will take the other one away and we do it. I don't care which one you choose as long as you choose one. There will be no more retakes, no more second chances. You will say the line. I will record the line. Then we're both outta here. OK, Jim?"

"OK, Morey. I'm ready."

"Right. I'm going to talk you through the two options. Here's Option 1. 'Space: the final frontier -

Starship Enterprise - strange new worlds - new life - new civilizations, boldly to go where no man has gone before.' That means you have made a bold decision to go and you are going to deliver on it. Yes?"

"With you all the way, Morey. What's Option 2?"

"OK. Option 2 - here it comes. 'Space: the final frontier. Ya-da-da ya-da-da blah-di-blah ... new life and new civilizations, to go boldly where no man has gone before.' Which means you're going, and wherever you're going, you're going there boldly and you're going to impress the crap out of every new life and new civilisation you happen upon. Capisce?"

"Capisce."

"Jim. I can hear a scratching noise. Are your scratching something?"

"I'm just crossing out the words I'm not going to read. Like you said, there will be no more retakes. This will make sure I get it absolutely right."

"Well can you just stop it please? Now? Just let Rose-Marie take away the one you don't need. You and your laid-back Canadian-ness! Are you ready?"

"I am ready, Morey."

"Has Rose-Marie gone?"

"She's gone."

"OK, Jim. This is it - the final take. Give me your intro to the Starship Enterprise mission statement in THREE-TWO-ONE-MARK."

"Space: the final frontier. These are the voyages of the Starship Enterprise. Its five-year mission: to explore strange new worlds, to seek out new life and new civilizations …"

…

…

"Jim? JIM? Screw! The bastards have finished me early. There should be another minute – minute and a half. Who can I ring?"

But that was it. We really we're finished. The doors would burst open any second and the lights would go out. Then the concierge would be round to escort me from the building. So I'm stuck with what I've got. The admirals aren't going to like it. Not one bit. Jim. I am sure, was already out of there

You know what I think? I think he did this deliberately. I think he quite deliberately blew this whole session just to get his own way. That's what makes him a starship commander, I suppose. That's what makes him Canadian

God damn you, Canada! God damn you all to hell!

WORLD PEACE AND 'INTERNATIONAL RELATIONS'
A Fake History of an Artist

Being the most famous artist in the world in 1950, the most influential artist, in some views the most important artist, still did not shield him from bad experiences - as Pablo Picasso was about to find out. In the previous year, he had accepted an invitation from his old friends, the Partisans for Peace, called the World Peace Council, to a conference they had organised in England in November. Picasso had gladly said 'yes' to the invite, as had many other prominent figures of the radical left all over the world. The world, Europe in particular, was recovering from that terrible war against the Fascist regimes, many though not all of them now defeated. Bringing people together to strive for international peace

was important: this is what Picasso believed. So a conference to promote the peace movement was important too

The British government, the most socialist the country had ever elected, did not seem to agree. Prime minister Atlee tried to stop the event. He considered it subversive, a material threat to the fragile, barely-formed post-war Western entente. He turned to his Home Office and his Foreign Office. They refused visas. They rejected many delegates before they had even arrived in the country. They rejected Frederic Joliot, a French physicist who was Marie Curie's son-in-law. They rejected Dmitri Shostakovich, revered Russian composer whose work had so recently been denounced by Soviet officials for its so-called *formalism* which was thought to be decadent and Western. But they failed to turn away Pablo Picasso. This left him feeling adrift and alone in a place he did not know: it left him feeling frankly a little bit ridiculous: had he known the word, he would have felt a little daft

Nevertheless, the great Pablo, having travelled to England, went on via London to Sheffield, the city hosting the conference, where he joined the depleted assembly. During his short stay in this steel city, after making his speech in the City Hall, he did three things that were perhaps worthy of note

First, he ate at Butler's Dining Rooms, close to the city's university. Butler's has long ago disappeared but it is still very fondly remembered by older citizens. His menu choice there is not recorded but the house specialties were, depending on the time of day, a greasy bacon breakfast or, at lunchtime (dinnertime in local parlance) a meat and potato pie prepared and cooked on site, and served with the legendary Henderson's Relish, brewed and bottled barely a quarter of a mile away

Then, he performed his party piece, a lightning sketch. It is often claimed that the sketch, a dove of peace, was drawn on a napkin in Butler's. But a napkin in 1951 in this northern city's leading greasy spoon? It seems unlikely. Serviette maybe. Nevertheless, the drawing was done and was presented with all ceremony to the organisers of the peace conference who use it as their logo even today

Last, he spent a night in Sheffield's Grand Hotel - a night he shared with a local girl known to him only as Pauline. Job done and payment made, the old roué may never have thought of her again had he not found a tiny slip of paper in his coat pocket as he travelled back to his home in Provence, to his lover Françoise, to their children Claude and Paloma. He read the note: he read what he took to be the girl's surname - G-U-Y-T-E. He could not imagine how that would be pronounced. He read it over and again before rolling the note between his fingers and his thumb. He lifted his hand to launch the paper pellet and - and - and then he placed it back in the pocket where he had found it

As Picasso walked through the door of their home at Vallauris, Françoise ran to embrace him and he spoke to her - but to his shock, he addressed her not in her native French or his native Spanish, but in the very northern

English he must have acquired during his brief time in Sheffield. "Nah then, Françoise."

He felt confused, felt his lover's body stiffen. He tried again. "Nah then, Françoise. Calm thi'sen," and again he paused

And again he tried to speak. "Ar'tha or'reight, love? 'Ow's t'kids? 'Ow's our Paloma an' our Claude?"

Françoise pulled away. She could not conceal her disappointment, her contempt, and she addressed him - in French. "Son nom? Quel est son nom?" she asked him curtly. "Seule une femme pourrait vous faire parler de cette manière très étrange." There had to be a woman in this somewhere, she felt: there inevitably was when he acted strangely. She wanted to know the woman's name

Much as he might have wanted to, he could not conceal his guilt from Françoise, whom he truly loved, but his bizarre new dialect made him very uncomfortable. "Look Françoise. I know I sound reyt funny, like. I am'pt bin gone a week, an' I am'pt got t'foggiest what it is what's mekkin' mi talk like this. It's reyt that thi' were a woman - well a girl. Pauline. Shi were pretty enough, but shi wer' just a lass. It din't mean nowt. But now ah'm talkin' like this, an' ah don't like it any mooer than tha does

"Look - it'll be Christmas in a couple o'weeks - reyt? Let's get that o'er an' done wi', then ah'll go back to Sheffi'ld an' sort it all aht."

Françoise looked into his eyes. There were tears in her own and she let the artist kiss them away. She wanted to believe him. She wanted to believe him. She wanted to believe him

Pauline was glad the letter arrived on the day it did, a Saturday when she wasn't at work, and that she had found it before anyone else saw it. A foreign stamp was not something that fell through their letterbox often - ever. Questions would be asked, and answers would have to be won from her, no matter how she might resist. Even if the legend *République Française* on the stamp were not enough to alert her, and it probably would not be, there was only one possible source of a communication for her from overseas - that man she'd spent the night with in the Grand Hotel. When she had scribbled out her name and address, then dropped it into his pocket, she could think of nothing more romantic than to hear back from the old, foreign gentleman who had been so kind, so exciting - so Continental. She ripped the letter open and read it, but much had changed in the weeks that had followed their encounter

"Polly?" Pauline and Polly were best friends
"What?" Polly asked. The two had met on their first day at school in 1938 and had stayed loyal to each other ever since, even in the difficult period during the late war years when Polly had dipped in and out of school whilst her mother had tried to claim her back from her foster home

"I need thi to do mi a reyt big favour, Polly. Say tha'll do it. Please."

By the end of the war though, Polly's mother had given up. She was expecting again anyway and was now going to devote herself to her new family. Polly was glad. She liked her foster parents, who were both very patient with her. They needed to be: Polly was quite a girl

"Tha'll 'aff'ter tell me worr'it is. I'm not doin' owt that'll get me into trouble at oo'am."

Pauline confessed to her friend about the night she had spent with the foreign gentleman: she'd thought he said he was Spanish but the letter - she handed the letter to her friend - seemed to have come from France

Polly looked at the envelope, the stamp, the florid, looping handwriting, and her jaw dropped. "What? Yer lerr 'im …"

"Yeah. An' 'e g'en mi ten bob."

"Tha' toll'd me tha'd stopped aht wi' Cyril." Cyril was Pauline's young man, her fiancé since three nights previously when they had 'got engaged'. Polly read the letter. "So - what's this favour, then? What's tha want me t'do?"

The letter had told Pauline that Mr Picasso was coming back, that he would arrive in two days' time, that he wanted to meet her again, that he felt they had some unfinished business

"I can't go and meet 'im. Not nah Cyril's asked me to marry 'im. Tha'll 'ave to go an' see 'im fo' me."

"It's thee 'e wants to see, not me."

"Aw go on, Polly. Cyril'd kill me."

"'E wun't. 'E's reyt gentle, your Cyril. 'E wunt 'urt a fly."

"'E'd 'urt me if 'e caught me doin' it wi' a Frenchman."

"I thought tha said 'e were Spanish."

"Dun't marrer worr 'e is."

After the briefest pause, Polly said – in some alarm, "Tha dun't expect me to do it wi' 'im, does tha?"

"We-eyy - tha'd be or'reyt. Tha'rt not gerrin' married."

Polly's face paled just a little. "It'll not be or'reyt if I catch a babby though, will it?"

"Oh just tell Freddy it's 'is."

Freddy was Polly's young man. "Thee tell Cyril it's 'is."

"Come on, Polly. Ah thought tha' wer' mi best mate."

"Ah'm not tellin' Freddy owt. 'E wun't believe us, anyroo'ad."

"Why?"

"Becos," and here she did her best to adopt a superior, posher tone, "we 'ave never done it. Not prop'ly done it."

Pauline couldn't hide a smirk. "Wha-at? But tha wants to, dun't tha?"

"'Coo'urse. But 'e's too scared on 'is mam. She dun't like me anyroad, and she wants to bust us up. She proper freightens me, shi does."

"Yeah but tha'd marry 'im, wun't tha?"

"She'll never lerr us."

"If tha wer' 'avin' 'is babby, she wun't stop thi."

"But ah'm not 'avin' 'is babby."

"Look - all ah'm askin' is fo' thi to go an' meet this bloke. 'E might not what to do it - not wi' thee anyroo'ad. But if th'art worried, why dun't tha just do it wi' Freddy t'neet and then it wain't marrer. Wor'ever 'appens, tha'll be or'reyt."

Waiting outside the Three Tuns, the pub across the road from the hotel, Polly felt very exposed - almost in danger. What on earth had possessed her to agree to this, she could not imagine. She would make sure that bloody Pauline paid for it for years to come

She saw a policeman walking towards her. She began to be frightened, but he walked by towards the police box outside the Town Hall. When he disappeared inside, she felt a wave of relief pass over her, and she decided she'd had enough. She wasn't going to wait here just to get Pauline bloody Guyte out of trouble. And then he appeared - on the steps of the hotel. A short man, a bit tubby, in a fawn sort of raincoat with a beret on his head - definitely not a Sheffielder, not looking like that

Screwing up all her courage, she walked across the road and addressed him. "Mester Picasso?"

The man turned and asked, "What's up, love?"

All her courage drained away. Whatever she had expected of someone called Picasso, a Frenchman or a Spaniard, an artist - whatever he was supposed to be - this was not the voice it would have used. "Are you Mester Picasso?" Her voice was trembling - just when she really wanted to sound cleverer than she thought she actually was

Picasso noted this and asked, in tones as kindly as he could muster in his still unaccustomed voice, "Aye lass. What can I do fo' thi?"

"Pauline's not comin'." She was blurting the words out rapidly. "Shi sez shi's gerrin' married an' shi dun't want to see thi."

"Gerrin' married?"

"Aye. T'Cyril. Thi've known each forra couple o' years an' it were bound to 'appen sooner olse later." She was speaking more normally again now, and it was some comfort

"Well bloomin' 'ummer. That's a turn up, in't'it? Gerrin' married. Pauline."

For seemingly long moments, though probably less than a minute, an obstructive silence stood between them, then the artist spoke again. "Tha must really like her to come an' do 'er dirty work forr 'er like this. It must 'a' bin a reyt errand for'a little lass like thee."

She peered up at this old man from under her eyebrows. For some reason, she felt she wanted to spend more time with him, to ask him why a Frenchman or whatever he was sounds like he has lived all his life in Sheffield, and was he really as famous as Pauline had made him out to be. But she couldn't think how to achieve that. "It weren't easy, tha'rt reyt."

"Then lerr us buy thi a drink, luv. In 'ere?" He indicated the pub door

"Thi wain't let me in. I'm only just turned eighteen a few days ago."

"Then p'raps - an' on'y if tha dun't mind - we can go an' 'ave a drink in t'room – my room - 'ere in t'otel."

This sounded exciting. She had never seen the inside of a hotel, especially not The Grand Hotel. "No funny business though."

"What's thi name, luv?" She told him. "Then no funny business, Polly," and he winked at her

At the back door of the hotel, Mr Picasso engaged in a conversation with a youngish man in a battered uniform that really should have been worn by someone with a much larger frame. The older man's hand disappeared more than once inside his raincoat, then emerged again, almost as if he had been trying to find something in an inside pocket that was then passed to the younger man. Polly really didn't understand what was happening, nor could she understand the mumbled conversation. Odd words registered, but no sense. Suddenly though they were ushered through the door, past the young man's cubicle and to a tightly winding flight of stairs

Polly sat back in the large armchair - poshest chair she'd ever sat in. She lifted her glass of sherry and looked across at him. "Cheers!" Sherry was the only drink she could think of that wasn't beer or shandy, and she didn't like those

"Salud!" Picasso said in return

"That din't sound very Sheffi'ld."

He came and positioned himself carefully on the arm of the chair, a glass in his hand. "Din't, did it?

"Look - summat funny 'appened to me when I were 'ere befoo-er. Like I took summat away wi' me that weren't mine to tek." He looked down into her deep brown eyes, as she looked up into his equally deep brown eyes. "P'raps ah've had to come back to le'ave summat t'mek up f'r it."

Pablo Picasso walked back into his home in Vallauris, Provence, in the middle of January. Françoise did not rush to greet him. Instead, he spoke to her. "Je suis chez moi, Françoise. Estoy en casa. Te he extrañado mucho. Je t'ai tellement manqué. S'il vous plaît venez m'embrasser. Por favor, ven y bésame. Bésame mucho." He told her he was home. He told her how much he had missed her. Ella lo besó. Elle l'embrassa. She kissed him.

In a brightly lit but drably decorated office, in March 1951 in Sheffield, Freddy took Polly to be his lawful wedded wife and Polly took Freddy to be her lawful wedded husband. In October, a son was born in the City General Hospital - and he had Polly's deep brown eyes

But tha'll never guess what! 'E din't 'ave both 'is eyes on't same side on 'is 'ee'ad! Thi were one on each side on 'is noo'as. Jus' like wor'it's s'posed t'bi

CAN'T BUY ME, LOVE
The Fake History of a Phone Call

The front door closed with a loud bang and a click of the latch, then a voice rang out from the living room. "Is that you, Freda love?"

"Yeah, dad. It's me. I'm back. Shall I put the tea on?"

Her dad replied, "That can wait. There's a message for you next to the telephone. The bloke said it was urgent. Are you planning a holiday or something?"

"No." The question meant nothing to her. "What's the message?"

"It's written on the pad. If you're not planning a holiday, then it must be something to do with the bloomin' fan club. It's a message to ring somebody back – somebody in London. And you can make sure those layabout mates of yours pay for it if it's to do with them. They can afford it, after all."

Freda's *layabout mates* were in fact The Beatles. Freda Kelly was secretary of The Beatles' fan club worldwide.

She was also secretary to the group's manager Brian Epstein. Over time, she had got used to the constant digs her dad made about the group. She knew he knew really that they all worked very hard, but like a lot of people of his generation, he was a bit unsettled at the way the world was changing. He didn't think pop groups and lads growing their hair long and girls wearing mini-skirts *that nearly showed you their ...* - always petering out at that point - was what the country had fought the Second World War for. *And* won, he always added. *And* won. She was also used to getting letters and phone calls from strange people and strange places, so another one didn't surprise her at all. Only when she began to look into it did this one felt a bit extreme. At least it did when her dad had helped her decipher his writing and she realised who had called her

She had taken the note into the living room so she could sit down next to him at the dinner table and, when he put *The Echo* down, tell her what it said. "So what do BOAC want with me? What did they say?" she asked, not really expecting any sensible sort of response

He didn't do details very well, not even important ones. It was just a name and a phone number scrawled on the writing pad. But he did come up with one good suggestion. "When you ring him back, this bloke, Guthrie or whatever he's called, tell the operator to reverse the charges. That way, if he accepts the call, you'll know how serious he's being."

She dialled 100, the operator answered and Freda told her she wanted to make a reverse charges call to BOAC in

London to speak to a Mr Guthrie – someone called Giles Guthrie. Before the operator could respond at all, Freda had also added her name and, probably more importantly, The Beatles' name. Suddenly it seemed the operator couldn't do enough for her. The response from the BOAC telephonist was of the same order – professional, but with just that little hint of excitement that she could not hide. She had been warned to expect the call, it seemed, and told she should put it straight through to him

Now Freda was starting to be impressed. She knew well from experience how good the mere mention of the Fab Four was at opening doors that remained firmly shut to most folk, but even for them this was good. She had seen the man she was about to speak to – *Sir* Giles Guthrie, not just plain mister – on the telly. He wasn't as famous as John and Paul and George and Ringo were: she didn't think he was, anyway. But he was famous. He was some sort of important businessman, and he had been brought in by the government because BOAC was in financial trouble and needed someone to shake it all up a bit, as her dad would no doubt have put it. It was a complicated business story and she really didn't understand it. But here she was *returning his call*. That was a phrase Brian used when he had missed someone ringing him up, and it sounded important. It made her feel important to be doing it

It was still a shock, though, to hear the telephonist announce her. "Miss Kelly for you, Sir Giles."

He thanked the telephonist then launched straight into, "Thank you for calling me back so promptly, Miss Kelly. I'm glad you got the message. I wasn't sure if the gentleman I spoke to was quite understanding me."

"That was me dad. He can be a bit vague sometimes, but he wrote the important stuff down ...." She then paused ever so slightly before asking, "What am I supposed to call you? Please forgive me for asking, but this is all new to me. Is it *Sir Giles* like the girl on the phone just did?"

"Oh, there's no need for formalities. Giles will be perfectly sufficient."

"OK then, Giles." She paused again. "Even that sounds a bit fancy. I don't think I've ever spoken to a Giles before. We don't get very many of them up here."

"It is a little old world, isn't it? Even without the *sir* on the front, it sounds rather like a medieval knight. But it is the name my mother and father chose for me, and I wouldn't want to distress them in any way."

"So – Giles. What can *I* do for *you*?" she asked, stressing both pronouns very firmly

"I've been trying to contact Mr Epstein's office, but I have got no answer."

"No. It's been one of those days today. Brian's had to dash off to London because he's got some important business down there that needs to be sorted out. I had to take care of some things in town at this end too, so we weren't there."

"Well I then tried to contact Mr George Martin at his recording studio. He wasn't available either, but his office told me you might be able to help me. They gave me your home number. I hope you don't mind that I rang you there."

"That sort of depends on what you're going to ask me."

"Quite right, Miss Kelly. Quite right."

As the businessman cleared his throat, Freda chipped in, "And if I'm calling you Giles, you'd better start calling me Freda."

"Thank you – Freda. I take it that you've heard the news about the boys, The Beatles. Especially about Mr Starr."

"Yeah – poor Ringo. Imagine getting tonsillitis just when you're supposed to be setting off on another world tour."

"It is difficult to think how he must feel. But it is the very subject I would like to talk to you about."

"You're not going to tell me you play the drums, are you, Giles?"

Polite laughter was heard at both ends of the call. Sir Giles was first to speak again. "I think my pretensions to musicianship ended a very long time ago. I struggled for two or three years with the violin and the piano, but it just wasn't for me. My mother was terribly disappointed but I was always more interested in sport, cricket especially."

"Shame. I was just trying to imagine the fun Pete Murray or somebody would have on *Top of the Pops* introducing John, Paul, George and Sir Giles."

"I imagine my sons would have a great deal of fun with that thought as well. Fortunately for me, and for everyone, I believe the vacancy has already been filled."

"Jimmie Nicol, you mean? I haven't any idea if he can do the job, but George Martin thinks very highly of him and he should know."

"I'm sure Mr Martin is right. As you say, he should know. But the fact of the personnel change still remains and, no matter how good Mr Nicol may or may not be, when the group sets off on tour, and until such time as Mr Starr is recovered and able to re-join the ensemble, it will not really be The Beatles that people are going to see, but three quarters of them plus a stand-in."

"Not really The Beatles? What are you getting at? It was John and Paul who started The Beatles. George came along after. Ringo only joined the group when Pete left. Not that I'm saying anything wrong about Ringo. Ringo is absolutely great and as much a part of The Beatles as anybody. And he's a really good friend of mine too. But whoever's in the group, if John and Paul say it's The Beatles then it's The Beatles. And I'm sure all the fans in Australia and America and all the other places they're going will all feel the same."

"Oh Miss Kelly – Freda – please don't be offended. It isn't my intention to say anything bad about The Beatles. I simply want to establish contact with them, or with their representative, so I can discuss what I think will be a mutually beneficial business opportunity. And so far, you are the only representative I have managed to get hold of."

"Well I can't help you on any of the business arrangements, but as well as being secretary of the fan club, I'm also Mr Epstein's secretary and I'm sure I shall be speaking to him in the very near future – quite possibly this evening. So if you want to give me some idea of this – what did you call it? – mutually beneficial business thingie, then I can pass it on to him and he can decide whether or not he wants to pursue it."

"Thank you, Freda. That is all I can ask."

What followed was several minutes of a mainly one-sided telephone conversation in which Sir Giles Guthrie, from his office at Gatwick, outlined his business idea and Freda Kelly, perched on the seat of the telephone table in the hall of her parents Liverpool home, scratched shorthand notes with a far from adequate ballpoint pen in the writing pad they left by the phone for just such a purpose – though rarely were the notes on the pad as copious as these. Only occasionally did the secretary interrupt the businessman's flow to ask for clarification of an unfamiliar or unheard word or phrase. Then, suddenly, she didn't shout down the phone, though it wasn't far from a shout. "You what?"

The businessman, taken aback, replied, "I beg your pardon, Freda?" It was not within his experience to be so directly or so forcefully challenged by a secretary

"Did you just suggest that The Beatles should change their name?" Her professionalism was stretched to breaking point by what she considered a stupid, outrageous suggestion

"Not change their name, no, Freda. The Beatles, as I am sure you would be the first to tell me, are The Beatles. Nothing in the world could change that, and no one in his right might would ever attempt such a thing." Not since his earliest years as an aviator had he felt so pressing a need to explain himself and seek approval, certainly not since assuming his baronetcy at the end of the war. "It would simply be to assume a new name for a particular purpose and for a brief time. It would be more like a joke than anything. Aren't The Beatles supposed to be renowned for their sense of fun?"

Having been very impressed by him at the start of their conversation, Freda was fast starting to mistrust, even disdain, Sir Giles flippin' Guthrie's attitude. "But what would be the point of it?" she asked. "What would anybody gain?"

"I can answer that question for you in a single word," Sir Giles told her. "Publicity. The Beatles need publicity. BOAC needs publicity. Everybody who is in business, whatever business that might be, needs publicity."

"I still don't see what the point of it would be. Why would it be good publicity for The Beatles to pretend to change their name? People would think they'd gone daft."

"Let me try and explain, Freda. The Beatles named themselves The Beatles presumably for a variety of reasons. And one of those reasons was, I imagine, was to set them apart from all the other pop groups playing up there in Liverpool, in the Cabin …"

"You mean the Cavern."

"Yes. Sorry. The Cavern. I did know that. But my point is that, whatever they original reasons may have been, it was a decision that worked. It worked very well indeed. With their name, as well as with their songs and their personalities and everything else that goes to make them what they are, they have become the most famous and most popular pop group in the world today. In fact, they have become a real symbol of Britain, as important and as recognisable as the red buses in London and policemen's helmets, and – yes – even as famous as the Crown Jewels. And whilst there are millions of people round the world who don't like your friends, there are millions more who do

"But fame is a thing that, whilst hard won, is easily lost. It takes a great deal of work to ensure that it grows and stays ahead of all the other pretenders – the people, the other pop groups, who would dearly love to swap places with The Beatles and take over what they have got. Of course their talent will always be the most important thing to keep them ahead of these rivals. If they can keep on producing the songs that people want to hear, and keep on performing the shows people want to see, then that is a large part of the battle. And yet – and yet – not everyone who deserves to be famous will get to be famous, and not everyone who becomes famous will get to stay famous. Do you see what I'm saying, Freda?"

"I can understand it when you say you've got to work at your fame and look after it, just like you have to with anything in life that's worth having. What I don't see is how this publicity is going to do anything for The Beatles if they change their name and nobody knows who it is."

"I'll give you an example that might make it easier to understand. Do you remember those flight bags we produced at BEA last year?"

"What? You work for BEA as well then?" One man having jobs with two different companies seemed like an odd idea, but Freda was rapidly realising there were many things about the world of business she did not understand

"Yes. I'm a BEA director as well as BOAC."

"And you're talking about that flight bag that said The Beatles on it?"

"That's the one. What I am proposing is something very similar to that."

"I've got one of those bags. Brian gave it to me. But it just says The Beatles on the side – and British European Airways."

"But the BEA logo, the white letters in the red square, make part of the word Beatles. It was a very clever gimmick one of our publicity boys came up with. I thought so anyway."

"But it still says The Beatles no matter how much they've mucked about with the letters. What you're suggesting, if I'm understanding you, is a bag with the 'The Boactles' on it." She pronounced it as if *Boactles* really were just a single word

"I was thinking that we would pronounce it The B-O-A-C-tles." Sir Giles pronounced the company initials. "It gets the company name in correctly, you see, but still doesn't move it very far away from the proper name of the group."

"It all seems like a lot of work just for the sake of a few bags. And won't people just think you're copying what BEA did last year anyway?"

"Oh Freda. This has nothing to do with bags. They might make a nice souvenir, I suppose. I really hadn't thought of that, but what I am really after is a photograph, and a press story on the business pages of all the serious newspapers around the world. There are business editors across the globe who would dearly love to have an excuse to feature a picture of The Beatles on their pages, but they need a proper business story to attach it to. What I want to do is give them that story. We could take one of our planes and make the logo on it say The B-O-A-C-tles, in the same way the bag you've seen says The B-E-A-tles on the side. We then stage a photograph with The Beatles and some of our air hostesses in front of that logo, and mail the picture out. The combination of four famous young men and a bevy of pretty girls will be too much for all but the most hard-bitten news editor to resist."

"And is that all your air hostesses are to you? A bevy of pretty girls?"

"Oh I don't think we'll have any problem getting volunteers for the job. I'm sure most of our girls will jump at the chance of appearing in a picture with Paul and John and George and - - the new man. We might even have to hold some of them back."

"You could be right there. The lads can have that effect on girls, even on the ones you would think had more sense."

After the last few exchanges in which he thought he had been losing Freda's respect, Sir Giles now thought he had her back on side, enough perhaps to risk a cheekier question. "Do you have more sense, Freda?"

She was a bit shocked that he had asked her that. "What? Oh, there wouldn't be anything like that with me. We've all known each other far too long. We're friends. And I'm lucky enough to work for them. I wouldn't want anything to spoil that. Not anything."

"I'm very pleased to hear that, Freda." A more business-like tone was beginning to creep back into his voice. "And I really should explain the offer that BOAC is prepared to make to The Beatles and to Mr Epstein. In return for the photograph such as I have described, taken at Gatwick Airport when the group sets out on its tour in a few days' time, we are prepared to reimburse all the group's air fares incurred on their forthcoming world tour. I'm sure you can appreciate that I am offering a very substantial sum, Freda. I'm doing that because I expect BOAC to benefit very substantially from the publicity such a photograph will garner for us."

Freda did know just how much money was involved in air fares on the tour. She didn't make the bookings herself, but she did see the invoices, and the numbers were eye-popping. "You're offering to return all the money The Beatles are spending with BOAC?"

"Not just BOAC, Freda, but with all the other airlines too. It seems likely, having seen the itinerary when it was in the papers, that they will be flying with BEA or perhaps Lufthansa or KLM on the European leg, then with Qantas when they reach Australia, and when they're in the USA it is anybody's guess. But, on sight of all the invoices, BOAC will guarantee to reimburse the entire air flight bill for the whole tour. And not just for the group members either, but for the complete entourage."

"Well that does sound like a generous offer, Giles, and I will pass it on to Brian as soon as I speak to him. I think he probably will call me from his hotel this evening, so you may even hear back from him tomorrow."

With all the confidence of a battle-worn WWII flying ace, he felt he had now achieved his purpose, and could not resist adding, "Thank you, Freda. Thank you so much. I'm sure the task will be dealt with most efficiently and effectively. Now – is these something that BOAC can do for you? To show our gratitude for helping us with this issue?"

"No. You're all right, Giles. That won't be necessary."

He had not expected this rebuff. "But surely – a bright young thing like you – there must be somewhere you'd like to go, something new you'd like to experience. We could really show you a very good time …"

"I think you'd better stop right there, Giles. I'm just an ordinary girl doing her job. I get paid to do it and I enjoy doing it. And I know there's thousands of girls out there who would give everything they've got if they could swap places with me, so there's no chance I would put that at risk just for some jaunt offered to me by a posh bloke with a fancy title. The Beatles and Brian keep talking about moving down to London, but me dad won't let me go, so I'm sure he won't want me getting involved in any good times you want to show me. Whatever they might be. I don't think you've got anything you can offer me – *SIR* Giles. No. Stop right there. You can't buy me, love."

"He said what?" Mr Kelly was angry at what his tearful daughter was telling him

"He said I was a bright young thing, dad, and there must be something new I'd like to experience. He said he could show me a very good time."

"If I could get my hands …"

"Calm down, Mr Kelly. Calm down. There's no need to lose your temper over this." Paul McCartney was also in the Kelly's living room. He was there visiting Freda, just to say ta'ra before they set of on the tour. "It's The Beatles got Freda into this, so it's only fair that The Beatles should get her out of it. When we get home from the tour. I don't know how yet, and I don't know when, but me and the lads will find some way to get back at this bloke for you. Just leave it with us."

Freda remembered this conversation every time she heard The Beatles sing *Back in the USSR*

Flew in from Miami Beach – BOAC. Didn't get to bed last night. On the way, the paper bag was on my knee. Man, I had a dreadful flight

THE HAY WAIN
A Fake History of Art

It is the wagon in the painting that draws your eye, stationary as it is and just out of centre. The horses that should be pulling it are up to their fetlocks in the stream, taking a lazy and doubtless well-earned drink. The clue of course is in the title: of course the wagon is what the artist wants you to focus on

I have to confess that when I looked at the picture, looked at it properly for the first time in the flesh, so to speak, not in a magazine or on a tea-try but in the same room, my instinct was to add a caption. It was hanging there in its majesty in the National Gallery, and all I could think of was words to the effect of *'Hey Wayne! Be a good ol' boy. Come and gi' us a shove, will you? I've got meself stuck in the chuffin' river again.'*

But the thing I really want to know, need to know, is *why*. Why is this great big wagon, with its team of three powerful-looking horses still in harness, just standing there in the middle of the river?

They know lots of other things about the scene. They know, for example, where it is – on the River Stour sandwiched between Suffolk and Essex. They know so well where it is that they have built a visitor centre there, complete with gift shop probably. They know when it is – the finished article was first exhibited in 1821, so the preliminary sketches would have been made in the previous year or two. They know what time of day it was – at its first public showing, it was called *Landscape: Noon*. They even know who lived in the house you can see to the left of the wagon – Farmer Lott. Willy Lott, a tenant farmer, was born there and he died there and, according to the story, never spent more than four nights away from his home in his whole life

They even know – though not many other people seem to - that it was largely overlooked on its first public appearances in London. Only in 1824 at exhibitions in France did it start to gather the reputation it now enjoys. But maybe this is not the time to remind the English of any French role in their cultural history

Yet none of this satisfies me. If you look it up, there are conflicting theories about what the wagon is doing in the river, none of which seem to be held with any conviction. Perhaps the most logical thought is the one in Wikipedia, amongst many other resources. Wikipedia suggests that the driver of the wagon has taken it into the river quite deliberately and stopped there to allow the wooden wheels to rehydrate. It is harvest time, the wagon will have been out every day and all day as crops are gathered in, so the wooden wheels will have dried out substantially in the hot summer sun. But as wood dries, it also shrinks, and this means the metal rims that hold the wheels together cease to fit as tightly as they should. And nobody wants to see the wheels on the wagon shedding metal, not at the very time when they need to have it working every bit as hard as all the people have to. But like all sensible, plausible theories, this is a dull and boring one. I longed for something more stimulating, more exciting

Maybe, for example, there were three lads hard at work with their families in the fields, bringing home the harvest. Since it is unlikely they actually existed, we have no idea what their names might have been, but as I am pursuing this unlikely tale, I am going to call them Michael, Franklin and Trevor. Even though the Michael, Franklin and Trevor I am imagining were only ten and eleven years old, they had to join in with the work: only the very youngest and the very oldest were let off the harvest – them and the posh folk up the Manor

The harvest seemed to go on and on, day after tiring day, field after enormous field, wagonload after laden wagonload. But our lads had been hatching a plot: hatching it for a long time, they'd been. And now the time had come for them to try it out or forget all about it. They were sure it was going to work so they were going to try it, dammit. Only Trevor had actually said *dammit*, but that was Trevor for you

When they had asked if they could have a day off, their dads had said they were all old enough to join in with the men's work in the fields, and none of the men was having a day off so neither could they. But what our lads reasoned afterwards was that if, as their dads had all said, they really were old enough for the work, then they were also old enough to start taking a few decisions themselves – decisions about what was going to happen in their lives. They decided, as one, that they were old enough to take a day off from all the back-breaking slog that shifting hay for such long hours brought them. They reckoned they could sneak off with a couple of apples and a chunk of bread, maybe even a piece of cheese if they were lucky, and have a lazy day down by the river

"It's just a day off," Trevor had said. Trevor was always first to speak up, even when he had nothing worth saying – especially when he had nothing worth saying. "Who'd want to complain about us doing that, then?"

"I'm sure our dads would if they knew what we were gonna get up to." Michael was a touch more realistic and knew they were taking risks, but he giggled as he said it because he was no less brave. And brave was just how the boys saw themselves - three brave adventurers setting out to do something no one else would dare, or even think of. "But they're not going to know, are they? Not if we've spun the right yarns to them." Michael looked straight at Franklin as he said this

Franklin didn't say anything. He rarely said much: he trusted the other two. They had always looked after him, after all

The boys laughed, throwing their arms round each other's shoulders as they marched off together, eagerly anticipating the day ahead. And they really thought they never would be missed – not if the tales they'd told worked out the way they were supposed to. Each one had told his ma he'd been asked to go and help his friend's dad with a particularly heavy bit of the harvest – Trevor with Franklin's family, Franklin with Michael's and Michael with Trevor's. The families all knew each other, of course, and were always happy to do each other favours in the knowledge the favours would always be returned. But they always worked different fields in the harvest so there was no way anyone would find them out. The lads would all go home that evening looking like they had all worked another hard, back-breaking day. It was likely the families would all meet up in church come Sunday, but one day was much like another at harvest time so they relied on no one quite remembering who been where doing what on which day. The plan could not possibly fail

As they marched along, down towards the river, Michael started singing: "*When I was a bachelor, I lived all alone and worked at the weaver's trade.*" Trevor, as Michael expected, joined in – at least with the bits he knew. *"And the only, only thing as I ever done wrong was to woo a fair young maid."*

Franklin, to no one's surprise, didn't join in. He didn't know the words at all. He might have heard the song before, late at night when some of the men sang it after they had had a bit too much ale, or a drop o'something else as they called it. He knew it was a rude song, though he didn't quite know what was rude about it, or why. But when his pals set to singing about wooing a fair young maid, he started to blush. "Stop it, you two. Someone might hear you." What he was more worried about was his ma finding out they'd been singing about wooing young maids. And it wouldn't matter if he'd joined in or not: she just wouldn't like it. She'd give him what for. It would be worse even than what he'd get if she found out he'd skived a day off working at the harvest. Trevor and Michael started laughing at him, and then they started singing again – at least they tried to. But laughter got the better of them. And Franklin laughed too. He knew he was a bit wet sometimes, but his ma did scare him

In this way, the adventure stretched out before our three lads as they strode determinedly down towards the river - one singing his head off, one alternately mumbling and shouting when it got to the bits he knew, and one not singing along, but at least not blushing any more - and even he was trying to memorise the words, if only to see if he could find out what they meant. Then suddenly something stopped them in their tracks – something they could not have expected, something that sent a thrill right through them

What they saw was Farmer Lott's great big wagon, the one he used to help shift the hay and all the other stuff everyone was out gathering in the fields. There it stood, its reins looped loosely round a tree, its team, all in harness and ready to go, munching contentedly at the grass - but with nobody in sight, nobody at all watching.

The three lads looked at each other with big round eyes. They had wanted an adventure, and what adventure could they hope for that would be better than a joy ride in the wagon old Farmer Lott had been daft enough to leave there for them? It was just too good an opportunity

They obviously were not going to go far. They weren't daft like the farmer. And they weren't going to be in the wagon for long because surely old Willy Lott or one of his men would be back for it soon. And in case they didn't get it back in quite the right place, they would just have to remember not to tie it up. That way it would look like the reins had just fallen off the tree where the wagon had been left and the horses had wandered a bit. "We're probably doing them a favour if they did but know it." The others looked at Trevor. He was obviously romancing again, they both thought, but Michael had to ask him how. "It'll stop 'em from stiff'nin' up, a bit of exercise. The horses I mean," was his reply. "By rights, they should thank us." Franklin and Michael both shrugged

In no time, they were up on the wagon. Franklin had thought that, as the really sensible one, he should drive. But as the sensible one, he it was he who thought of unfastening the reins from the tree – and by that time Michael had hauled himself up into the driver's position. Franklin thought about arguing the point, but realised quickly it would be a waste of time, and at least it wasn't Trevor, he said to himself, so he just handed them to his mate and dashed round the back of the wagon to bunk in ready for the ride alongside the other two. They were ready. Michael held the reins high, then gave them a serious shake and called out some meaningless syllable

And – nothing happened. The horses just kept on munching away

He went through the process again – and still nothing happened. After a third time, Michael began to feel a bit stupid. Trevor and Franklin were wondering what they could do to help make something happen when, without any warning that was apparent to the boys, the horses suddenly sprang into action and set off. They set off with such force that the three boys were quite startled. Trevor had not been holding on to anything and he fell over backwards as the wagon jerked forward, almost tumbling out of the open back. The other two had managed to stay on their feet, but both looked on in horror as the reins fell from Michael's grasp and disappeared beneath the horses. Now they had not a hope of bringing the charging horses back under control

But their fears lasted only moments since the horses, having seemingly bolted, stopped almost as suddenly as they entered the river. Here the horses took their ease and started taking long draughts of water. The friends exchanged glances, Trevor struggling to stand up again, and all three knew what they must do. They leapt down from the wagon and were off like a shot. They knew their only hope lay in getting back to the fields and trying to sneak back in amongst everyone as if they had been working all along. "Please let no one have seen us," Franklin muttered under his breath. "Please let no one have seen what we did." Not one of the three gave any further thought to what might have caused the horses to bolt in the first place

What they had not seen, but what the horses had obviously sensed, was the arrival of a solitary man. By his fine clothes, the lads would have labelled him a stranger, not knowing he had been born here, just as they had, and that, though he had moved away, he returned every summer. The man was in fact John Constable, the artist - though not yet the famous artist he was to become. He had returned home, as so often he did, for inspiration. He had chosen this particular spot, so close to his old home in East Bergholt, to begin a series of sketches preparatory to a work he had envisaged some time ago. Having chosen his spot, he set about arranging all he needed to carry out his task. He set up his folding wooden seat. He lay down his box on the ground so he could easily reach inside for paper, pencils, charcoal, for canvas and oils - and for the packed lunch he had brought. Then he took his seat and took in the scene before him. He thought it perfect, ideal for his purpose, and quickly he began sketching the wagon, for he knew enough of the demands of the harvest to realise it would not be left there idle for long. Soon a workman would arrive to take the wagon and put it to work moving the hay being gathered in as he sat there. But the workmen who did arrive were also quickly sketched into the scene. He was working so hard that, even when these men expressed surprise at find the wagon where they found it, it did not even for a moment occur to him to explain what he had seen the three young lads doing when he arrived

So began his preparatory work on what would become the work for which he is perhaps most famous the world over – the work we all know now as *Grand Theft Hay Wain*

BYE-BYE, BOBBY DARIN
The Fake History of a Song

Little is known about his life, save that it was a seemingly ordinary one lived entirely in the north of England. He was born at the height of the Second World War and grew up during its aftermath. The few documents that exist point to him having been a solitary man who worked in mundane, menial jobs, who had few friends, who never married, who left no children. The work for which his is now known around the world lay unpublished, undiscovered till after his death. Until now, it was not even known when he created the work

But a fragment of quarter inch reel-to-reel recording tape has been found in the archive of the Telegraph & Star, his local newspaper, presumably source material for a feature that seems never to have been published. It is the only first-hand material that sheds light on either the man or the work

The quality of the recording has been enhanced, but it remains very poor in places. We present here a transcript of what does exist as an insight into the creation of what has become one of the world's most popular songs

"… and anyway Friday night's always the same in there. Blokes who drink all week in the taproom will grudgingly stump up the extra tuppence a pint for concert room prices 'cos the missis is with them. Or the bird. And they'll have the Brylcreem on, and the suit – with the full watch and chain, some of 'em - and the shiny, shiny shoes as well. Oh, they really push the boat out on Fridays, some of 'em

"I get to spend my Friday nights playing the piano and singing in there for most of them just to ignore – or for ten bob an' free beer to be more precise. Ha-ha. But then most times, once or twice in the night, there'll be that bit of a movement that I always recognise – the woman nudging the man, him trying to turn his back, big blokes usually – steelworkers, brickies, somethin' like that – desperate not to stand out from the crowd. Sooner or later though, and inevitably, he just has to give in. And his mates all grin as he wanders across to me

"Some of 'em do at least wait till I've finished whatever it is I'm playing, but some of 'em don't even bother to do that. Either way though, they ask if I can do a request – *it's the wife's favourite and it's her birthday*, or *the girlfriend's got the record and she's always playing it*. Summat like that. Asking the piano player for requests isn't something men round 'ere want to do, and neither is bothering to remember the title of the song quite often. You wouldn't believe the rigmarole we have to go through sometimes. It can be a right palaver

"I remember once this bloke coming across to me. I'd spotted him earlier – looked about forty but was trying to act and dress half that. The woman he was with – the girl he was with – certainly looked half that, if that. But it's 1962. They're putting men in space so anything's ..." CRACKLES "... then he asked me if I could do that *Hot Banana* song as he called it. I don't know any *Hot Banana* songs, and I told him. He told me I did, that it's the one where they keep singing *hot banana hot banana* between all the lines

"*Well I thought it might be when you said it*, I told him. I tried to make this sound like a friendly joke, not just sarcasm. *But that doesn't help me. Has it got any other words? Do you know how the tune goes? Do you know who it's by?* But we got nowhere. Then with a sort of scowl and a flick of his head he called the girl over and told her I didn't know the *Hot Banana* song and she'd have to explain. She cracked out laughing (which sounded like someone had just spilled a bag of ball bearings on to a steel sheet) and told me it was *Teddy Bear*, the Elvis ..." CRACKLES "...*Banana* was apparently just what she and her sister would sing in between the lines. It made them laugh apparently. This is the kind of audience I can get, but I could imagine what she meant. Anyway I gave them *teddy Bear*, complete with *hot bananas* in all the places where I thought they ought to be - and they didn't even listen.

89

Just kept up their conversation. Mercifully it is a short song

"And there are worse types – the ones who do pay attention, the ones who know a bit and think they know the lot. One particular night, it was a night when everything had been going well, when I'd done my Frank Sinatras and my Nat King Coles, and some rock'n'roll stuff for the kids, I even did *Singing in the Rain* for old Martha, one of the regulars. This was a departure for her. Usually she wants *Don't Laugh at Me Because I'm a Fool*

"*Give us a night off, Martha*, I'd pleaded and she had done for once. That's how I got Gene Kelly not Norman flamin' ..." CRACKLES "... knocked off for a while. Needed to go to the lav anyway. Needed another pint. Needed to rest my voice before giving them something a bit special, something I'd been working on. While I walked across the room, I spotted the three of them. Hair a bit long. Suits a bit scruffy. One of them wasn't even wearing a tie. *Dunno what the world's coming to*, I remember thinking

"Anyway, when I got back to the piano, there they were, pints in hand, standing almost in touching distance of my stool. I looked at the big clock up on the wall – five and twenty to ten. I was due to knock off at quarter past, five minutes before the landlord would ring last orders and they'd all make a mad rush for the bar. Maybe it wouldn't be too bad." LOUD CLICKING - AT THIS POINT THE TAPE BROKE. FRAYED ENDS WERE REMOVED AND THE TAPE WAS SPLICED BACK

TOGETHER. "… this wispy moustache, trimmed to look like Errol Flynn I supposed, asked me if I did requests

"Well, my heart sank. He asked me if I knew that Bobby Darin one and it sank further. That *Le Mare* or whatever it's called – he called it that, *le mare*, like it was a horse. My heart stopped sinking and came to rest on the sea bed. That really is what it felt like. And it settled gently into the soft sand it found there. Sorry. Am I getting' a bit poetic for you?

"Anyroad. He couldn't have asked me for anything worse. Not on that night. I certainly knew the song he meant – knew it very well. In fact, it was so nearly the very next song that I planned to give them. But I'm sure that what this bloke really wanted was Bobby Darin's *Beyond the Sea*, not Charles Trenet's *La Mer* in French, and especially not with my own English translation stuck on at the end

"I'd always loved the French song, ever since I first heard it on the radio when I was about twelve. I was doing a bit of French at school back then, not enough to know what the song was about - not really - but enough to make me interested. It just sounded really intriguing. Then when Bobby Darin's version of it came out, it nearly drove me crackers at first. I knew that, whatever Charles Trenet had been singing about, it wasn't what Bobby Darin was singing

"I never forgot the song – often used to think about it. It was the kind of thing you used to get on *Housewives' Choise* or *Family Favourites* every once in a while

"Then, one day, I just had an idea, though where it came from I couldn't tell you. I went down to the music shop in town - the one by the Goodwin Fountain, near the Town Hall - and I bought myself a copy of the sheet music with the words in French. The bloke in the shop seemed quite pleased - not the kind of thing they get asked for very often. He had to go in the back and was gone nearly five minutes

"I then spent weeks working on my own translation of it with what little French I remembered from school but hadn't used for years, and poring over the little Collins French-English/English-French dictionary my auntie had bought me one Christmas: *what a useless present* I'd thought at the time. I was glad of it now though. I'd gone over it time after time, and when I finished it earlier in the week I decided I would give it a great unveiling in the pub – a world première if you like

"He really is one for imagery, old Charles Trenet. And it wasn't all soppy love stuff like in the Bobby Darin one is. His song is about the sea, but also about the weather and sheep and little houses and reeds growing in ponds. And it all makes sense – just in a completely barmy and very French sort of way. And it's funny too: people don't think about the French having a sense of humour, but Charles Trenet has one

"I'd even finished up buying a school exercise book and drawing up grids on the pages so I could make sure all the words I wanted would fit properly, long and short syllables in the right places to fit the rhythm of the song but still keep the sense and the feel of the French words.

And this young feller stood there telling me he wanted Bobby Darin and his lover who stands on …" CRACKLES

"I wanted to give him and his mates Charles Trenet and *La mer, qu'on voit* …" CRACKLES "… bet any money you like, even if these blokes could put up with it, that they were not going to be happy with *The sea – watch how the waves dance out there in the bay*. That's how my translation starts

"They didn't look at all as though they'd be up for anything that different – anything they'd never heard before. They actually looked like they'd all had a skin full. They looked like a bit of argy bargy with a piano player might be just what they wanted to send them out happy into the Friday night and off to the chip shop." CRACKLES "… did they? I wasn't sure. It might just have been me. Perhaps I was just looking for an excuse not to do my song. You do have to take a bit of flak, I kept on telling myself, if you're daft enough to try and perform in a pub: it's what happens sometimes. *Be brave,* I thought. *Be brave*

"In the French version, the words are there straight away. Lots of singers go even before the music starts, just the one beat – *Lah* rather than *La* – with whatever instruments only making their presence heard on *Mer*. I didn't do that. I just let the piano and the tune go their own way together, no words first time through, but lots of right foot to flesh out the sound and lots of twiddly bits to make sure it sounded like I meant business

"No sign of recognition from Errol Flynn who made the request: just a smile and a nod from Martha. At least she knew what it was. Then, far too soon for my liking, I wound up back at the start and I had to decide. And I did decide. And I went for it. I went with - Bobby Darin ..." CRACKLES "... *waiting for me*

"I was a yellow belly, I know. But why not? I certainly wasn't going to pick a fight with three blokes when any one of 'em could've made mincemeat of me. As I got further into it, it crossed my mind that it is actually a nice enough little song as it goes – if only they'd written a different tune for it as well, and not tried to pass it off. Then I wouldn't be dripping with nervous sweat and swearing at myself in my head. Then I wouldn't be despising myself for being such a coward. But at least I got a nod from Errol as I built up for the end. He'd finally recognised it

"There's a line near the end about *sailin'*. They were walking away, Errol and his mates

"And another line about *sailin'*. I followed them with my gaze as they walked across the room

"And another line about *sailin'*. I began to feel like I had actually won something

"One last line about *sai-ai-lin'*... And then it was bye bye, Bobby Darin – hello, Charles Trenet

"I launched straight into a much jauntier version of what I'd been playing, something very nearly music hall. And into the French words. And suddenly they were back, all three with a pint in each hand this time. It looked like they were the ones meaning business, like they were staying here till chucking out time. Two of the spare beers were plonked on the top of my piano, but Errol held on to both of his

"I kept singing - and they kept listening. They were bloody listening - to me. One of them was slapping the side of his thigh with his free hand as he drank deep from the pint in the other. They liked it, I think. I was almost disappointed when it got to the end, the line that at first I thought said, *'the sea has rocked my heart for life'* in French, but that I hoped I had finally made more sense of. Errol Flynn and his mates all clapped as I finished. Just the three of them, nobody else, but they actually bloody clapped. So I stood up and asked them if they knew what the song was about. Errol said he thought it must be same as what Bobby Darin sang, but I shook my head – I felt my confidence growing

"I told them I'd written an English version of the French words, not like the Bobby Darin which was a different song really, just with the same tune, and asked if they'd like to hear it. And they said yeah

"I sat down and for the third time launched into the intro of *La Mer* giving it the full verse without words again, but this time making it a much smaller, more intimate sound, no right foot at all and very little left hand. And next came the words …" CRACKLES "… my words

"*The sea – watch how the waves dance out there in the bay,*
twinkling with tiny silver lights that sparkle and shine
as the rain falls

"*The sea — greets summer skies, tends the little white lambs that float there like angels. The sea - takes care of us all under heaven*

"*Look here. See where the reeds grow tall down by the shore*

"*Look there. On high over houses, little birds soar*

"*The sea brings peace to all who stay here by the bay and, with its song of love, the sea has warmed my heart for a lifetime.*"

I was glad to get it over, glad to have done it and glad that …"

The tape ends abruptly here - not the recording, the tape, physically frayed. Obviously, there was more to the interview. How much, no one is likely ever to know

LIVE FROM SANTA'S SLEIGH
The Fake History of Christmas

Good morning viewers. It's now almost 6.00 am on Christmas morning and, here on UKTravelTV, we have a special seasonal treat for you. We have placed a camera in Santa's actual sleigh so that, now he's completed his UK run, we can go live to find the out some of secrets of just how he is able to deliver all those gifts to all those children all over the world in a single night. If everything is going to plan, he should be somewhere over the mid-West in the USA by now. So, let's go live to one of his little helpers who is going to provide a commentary on this unique television occasion

TINKLY INTRO MUSIC: JUST HEAR THOSE SLEIGH BELLS JINGLING, RING-TING-A-LINGLING TOO. COME ON, IT'S LOVELY WEATHER FOR A SLEIGH-RIDE TOGETHER WITH YOU

"What the hell did you pick this team for, Santa? I never saw such a crazy bunch of reindeer. If you don't rein 'em in, something bad's gonna happen. Poor old Plimft nearly fell out *back there over the ocean, and I'm sure the sack is gonna start spilling its load any time now." (Santa grunts)*

We're on? Right. We're on

Hi everybody. Merry Christmas and welcome to the fastest sleigh-ride you're ever gonna see. Meet the man – meet Santa Claus. (*Santa grunts*). He's the one you're waiting to see, after all

I suppose all you folks out there think you know about Santa Claus – jolly, apple-cheeked old guy with white whiskers and a fur-trimmed, bright red onesie who distributes gifts to all the kids of the world, all the ones on the good list, anyway – yeah? Well take it from me, folks - he ain't nothin' like that. No sir

C'm 'ere an' listen. Let me tell you a few things. First thing you should know is he got the job long before there was any such thing as licenses to drive sleighs. Now, there ain't nobody back at base who's got the guts to tell him he ain't up to it anymore. And he's happy to put these crazy reindeer up at the front of this rig and never even think about us poor sleigh-crew. (*Santa grunts*)

And he's the meanest, most cussed devil I ever met. Giving all that stuff away every year has made him so he hates people, especially the kids

...

OK. Yeah. Cameras rolling - got you

...

For the record, my name is Blift and I'm what you might call a Santa's Little Helper, same as Plimft back there. We're the ones who drew the short straws. We got the job of going out on the sleigh with the old schmuck, delivering all the kiddie stuff. And I guess Plimft's straw must have been just that teeny bit shorter even than mine 'cos at least I get to ride shotgun here up front with the big guy, but poor ol'Plimft - he's stuck at the back squealing

"Whoa - Santa. Be careful." (Plimft squeals) "This is Chicago remember. I know those guys in China and D'bai and wherever build taller these days, but that don't make these buildings any smaller than they always used to be. These reindeer you landed us with this year, Santa — they're gonna kill us all. And then we're never gonna meet the targets."

Oh yeah. Even Santa has targets to meet these days. But don't worry folks: this crazy sleigh-ride will just keep on rollin'

He got the reindeer from the same place in Finland we've been getting them for years, but I'm sure the guys in charge this year were Russians, and I just don't think they were reindeer farmers, somehow

But where was I? Oh yeah — Plimft at the back. *"Say hello, Plimft — we're on TV." (Plimft squeals)* He's got the tough job — making sure all this cheesy crap gets to all the right kids in all the right buildings as we pass by at speed. Of course, the job's not the same as it was — no more climbing down chimneys

...

Well - who has chimneys in the twenty-first century?

...

Nah, he has this app on his smartphone that makes the transfer. *"Show 'em your smartphone, Plimft. Oh — OK. I got it." (Plimft squeals)* But he still has to align everything and scan all the codes and make sure the broadband don't go down – and that don't leave him many hands to hold on with. You know what I'm saying?

It was easy enough to do all that back east where the signals are stronger. It ain't too bad even here over Illinois, but soon we'll be striking out into Iowa and Montana and the Dakotas, and believe me it's a different story out there

And I'm sure you all know the Dakotas bring a whole different set of issues for us Helpers

You what? You don't know? Well you're gonna learn some history here, boy. Just let me talk to the driver

"Hey Santa – you haven't forgotten that briefing we had the other day, have you?" (Santa grunts). That one about those gismos that some of the Chicago kids have gotten hold of – those drones? And that software that's supposed to let the kids tweak them so they can try and shake us down for all these presents?" (Santa grunts) "Yeah well - just watch out for them. If you see any, I can pick them off, but you have to tell me. Understand? And watch those buildings." (Plimft squeals)

...

What's so special about the Dakotas? Well, it's home to all us Helpers. It's where we came from nearly – ooh – just about eighty, eighty-five or so years ago. Most of us can get a little sentimental when we have to go back there, a little tearful even

...

You thought we came from the North Pole? Nah. That was just the story the PR team put out. I can see I'm gonna have to explain. Sit back folks and enjoy the story

Fake Histories

It's the name that's all wrong, you see – Santa's Little Helpers. Straightaway it gives the wrong impression. Always makes people think that we're little elves, or maybe pixies or gnomes or something. Well we're not. OK? We're Canotila

...

Canotila. CAN like in AmeriCAN. NO like what we Americans prefer to say to people from anywhere else in the world. TIL as in ... 9 till 5, which is not the kind of job we have. And LA as in – I dunno – OOH-LA-LA. Look I'm a magical being not a stand-up. What do you want?

"What the ...?" (Santa grunts). Look, bug guy, I know you think you're the greatest diver since Betty White and that right-hand you just pulled would make Lewis Hamilton proud, but you still have to squeeze the sleigh between all of the high-rises. (Plimft squeals. A lot.) Well - at least he's still there

"Jesus Santa!" (Santa grunts several times) "Oops – sorry – not tonight, OK. I understand. But just watch where you're flying, will you?"

So yeah – we're Canotila. We used to live in what you call North and South Dakota. That's not what we call it, but life's too short: we Canotila live a lot longer than you humans and there's still not enough time. We were the magical counterpart of the Lakota people. We used to take care of them

...

Never heard of the Lakota? They were part of the Sioux nation – yeah? Red Cloud? No? Black Elk? Crazy

Horse? Sitting Bull? Does nobody go to the movies anymore?

...

They don't make westerns anymore, you say? Crazy world you live in. Nearly as crazy as this guy who – AAAGH! – who is doing his darnedest to wrap us round a skyscraper!

Ah, don't worry about him though. He doesn't care these days. Hasn't cared for years. You know he's on the take, don't you? You know his famous list? The one he checks twice? That all the lady Canotila have to check for him more like. Well it's nothing to do with sorting the naughty kids from the nice kids. Nah. It's to sort the kids with the ordinary Joe parents from all the rich ones. Why else do you think it's always the rich kids get all the best presents?

"Hey Santa. Look. Down there. Torchgrove Apartments. Remember last time you and I did this run together, back when we still used to deliver in person, and somehow we'd made it into the wrong apartment and that babe had just got back from the gym?" (Santa squeals. Plimft grunts)

...

Yeah. Ok. We're on TV. I've not forgotten, but you can just cut that, can't you?

..

Live? Nobody said nothing about live. What time is it over there?

...

6.15 – in the AM? And there's kids watching? Well what kind of kids do you raise over there in England if they've nothing better to do than watch TV at 6.15 on a Christmas morning? Crazy place

Huh. So back to the Lakota then. When the European – settlers? Is that OK? Can I say settlers? When the Europeans started to arrive, most of the native peoples did not thrive. They did not prosper. They lost their homes and their lands. They lost the resources they needed to live. Pretty quickly there were nowhere near as many of them as there had been. But not the Lakota. Things definitely looked good for the Lakota. Somehow their numbers just grew

Now I don't want to claim the Canotila were the only reason for that. Lakota were always a pretty resourceful, resilient bunch of guys, knew the woods and the lakes, and how to work them. But we're a pretty powerful magical people too, that's all I'm saying

Then of course things got bad for everyone. The Wall Street Crash, the Depression, the Dust Bowl – powerful magic is one thing, but some European imports even the Canotila can't work against

"You OK back there, Plimft?" (Plimft squeals)

He's OK. Yeah – there we were staring at the Thirties and the old natural magic routine just wasn't cutting it. We needed a new outlet

We tried Hollywood. Nobody knew it then, not till about 1939, but those Munchkins had already got the place sewn up, like they still have. And then there were plenty of us who had superstitions about the movies too. I thought the others were all being stupid, but I was outvoted. Tell me this though. Have you ever heard of anyone losing their soul just because they worked in the movies? I don't think so

So Hollywood was out and we had to cast around. In the end, the answer came not from out west, but from the south – from Atlanta. We heard about this company that was looking to hire some magical people to work with this guy – Santa. (*Santa grunts*). They were giving him the full make-over. They got rid of the old-time European spookiness, the green robes, the leaves and twigs in his hair. They made him much more kid-friendly, with a happy bunch of nameless magical side-kicks – and the money was good, for him and for us. The advertising guys even wrote a special line for Santa to show he was a nice guy now

"Hey. Do it, Santa. Do the line. The kids over in England would love to hear the line." (Santa turns, looks at Blift and booms, "Ho-ho-ho!")

(Plimft squeals and squeals again) "BUT KEEP LOOKING WHERE WE'RE GOING! Jeez we – sorry – heck we nearly flew into those power lines

"You know if we make it through tonight, we really are gonna have to go and make some pretty powerful magic to thank somebody for it."

So we went to Atlanta. We submitted our tender. We got the contract. That was 1931 and the Canotila became Santa's Little Helpers under contract to Coca-Cola

Uuh - shouldn't have said that. You won't broadcast Coca-Cola's name, will you? I don't think they would want to be associated with this. Spoil the magic of the season, y'know. Not that it is magic, not really, but you know what they mean

...

Off the air? What do you mean off the air? The crack about the babe in the apartment? But I didn't say anything. I didn't tell you what she did for us. That would be worth taking us off the air for. Believe me - you'd go viral

(Santa and Plimft and Blift all squeal)

"SANTA — will you look where we're going. You're supposed to be driving this wreck!"

Look limey, we are busy here. We got millions of kids to make their day already. I am not going to let you spoil their dreams. But we got an agent and one of the biggest companies in the world behind us, so you can expect a phone call later today and if you can't come up with ...

CLICK

"Can you believe that? The jerk's cut us off. Santa — when we finish this, do you think you can detour these crazy reindeer by England ... for a comfort break? You know what I mean?"

(Santa grunts)

DISCARDED BY DICKENS
The Fake History of a Story Never Told

Ten days, ten whole days spent crossing the Atlantic Ocean on a steamship - this was not the master's idea of a pleasant way to travel, however modern and scientific the age we live in. This is what he told us, repeatedly

"Twenty-five years ago, I made the trip to America," he so often said, "and it presented me with what proved to be ten of the worst days of my life. Now Mr Cunard insists that his newest vessel, the *Cuba* he calls it, will be far more commodious and more stable than that earlier vile craft, but can I trust him? Really, I don't know."

He had made his earlier voyage aboard the *Britannia*. It had been the most famous steamship of its time, a marvel of the modern age, yet the master had been ill throughout the voyage. Now though he seemed to take rather a great and, to my mind, unnecessary delight in speaking of just how violently, painfully ill he had been on that occasion:

how the pail that was constantly between his knees had ruined all thoughts he had harboured of working whilst he crossed the mighty ocean. But perhaps this is just the foible of a famous writer

So bad had it been, he assured us, that he had gladly paid the extra expense for himself, his wife and their maid to come back from the Americas on a sailing ship called *George Washington*. They had sailed into Liverpool three whole weeks after leaving Boston, but he assured us all that he was a much happier man for it

Yet now he had consented to another sea voyage aboard another steam ship, to the self-same destination, and this time I was to accompany him and his wife. The master, of course, is a very important man and could ill afford not to go, as he would also remind us. But I was, and I remain, far from being important. As merely his wife's companion - I hesitate to say friend, whilst hoping I one day might - I did not know what I should do if the sea made me so ill and infirm that I failed to be a boon to both of them

I spoke, of course, to Catherine - to Mrs Dickens I should say - and she told me that the prospect of many thousands of pounds to be paid to him for speaking to audiences in the United States was drawing him back to that country at speed despite all possible discomforts, and that we were required to fit in with his needs

In the event, luck was with Mr Dickens on this occasion, as was his muse. Not only did we enjoy a peaceful and pleasant voyage on what he now saw was a much larger and more stable vessel, and in much fairer weather - in November rather than in January as on the earlier trip - but he was also able to complete a work in which he had been engaged for some considerable time

During our first weeks in the Americas, we stayed in Boston and there were many dinners, to some of which Catherine, Mrs Dickens, and I were invited, though to some we were not. My own most cherished moment in this period was meeting dear Mr Longfellow. How I have loved his *Song of Hiawatha*. It is dearer to me and more to my own taste than much of what Mr Dickens has written. I did not doubt though that it would make the master most unhappy to hear me say so, and I went out of my way to appear not to be favouring Mr Longfellow's company over any other's, lest my preference be remarked upon. Yet *Hiawatha* will be dearer still to me now, after I have met and conversed with its originator

In the day time, Mrs Dickens and I spent much time taking in the sights of the city where we stayed whilst Mr Dickens engaged himself in a seemingly endless series of meetings with Mr Fields, his American publisher. The object of these meetings, I was to learn over time, was to secure, for the first time in my master's career, first publication of one of his stories in America - before any should have chance to read it at home in England. This was the work he had completed whilst we sailed the Atlantic, a work which, as he told it, continued and complemented his earlier *A Tale of Two Cities*

It is a work about which he had become most passionate, telling as it does the story of the common people of Paris during those infamous revolutionary

Fake Histories

years. I have not read the work. None has save Mr Dickens himself and, I imagine, Mr Fields. Yet it seems that there is a matter of disagreement between them over the work. Mrs Dickens would certainly frown on me if she knew I had overheard a conversation between the two men, and would take great exception were she to know that I am about to share what I learned on that occasion. Indeed, neither do I have time for eavesdroppers, but in no way did I seek out the information I so gained. Yet, in the light of the events that have followed, I do believe the world must know what my master has been put through, what he has suffered. I shall here record their conversation verbatim, at least as closely to the actual words as I am able

Mr Fields at first appeared to heap praise upon the work, with words such as, "A rollicking tale, Charles. A great yarn yet again, and thought-provoking too. I have no doubt that this was your intention all along."

Naturally my master was happy to receive this praise for his latest creation. "Thank you, James. It is gratifying to hear such words from one whose opinions I have learned to hold in high regard. And you are right that, as well as being a teller of stories, I aspire to prick the conscience of my readers from time to time, in my own small way."

Soon enough though contention arose between them. "So there remains still just the one issue to be resolved." This was Mr Field speaking

"Oh James, please, not again." It became obvious to me immediately that my master was disappointed to have to deal again with the one issue, as Mr James called it. I knew well from a conversation between Mr and Mrs Dickens, and myself, as we had dined privately a few nights earlier, what the issue must be, and that Mr Dickens felt the matter had been dismissed. "Must I reiterate what I have already told you several times?" he asked, not a little impatiently

Mr Fields appeared to shuffle and splutter, but my master continued with great resolve. "I say again that I am an English writer writing in English in England, the land where the language was born and where it flourishes. To bow to your request for a change to the title of the work would be to flout the cultural superiority in the world which naturally belongs to the English race."

Mr Fields now changed his tack somewhat, attempting to appeal to Mr Dickens' logic. "But there is where the problem lies, Charles. The title of the work you are arguing for is not in English. It's in French - *Les Sans-Culottes*. Aside from a few folk down in Louisiana and a very, very few up in Maine, no American reader is even going to pick a book up with a title like that, a title in French. There are the Quebecers of course, the – ah - Québécois, but whilst they may like a French book title, they will hardly relish such a book whose text is almost exclusively in English

"No Charles, we need to give it a title that will work in our favour, a title that will draw the reader in, a title that they will understand. In short, Charles, we need a title that is in English."

At this, my master laughed a little - but not in any happy way. "And do you imagine, James, that the title in translation will be more to your liking, more likely to draw readers in? How do you think my readers will react to a book called *Those with No Trousers* or *Men without Trousers* or some such? I shudder to think what my readers might understand from such a title. How different the reaction would be in England. My readers there would not find any difficulty in simultaneously seeing a title in the French language as an indication of their own sophistication through ownership of such a book, whilst for those who understood it, the translation would merely confirm their already low opinion of Johnny Frenchman, as so many call our closest geographical neighbours

"At the same time, I can easily imagine some parts of your United States where the more extreme churchmen, for example, may well see such a book – a book called *Men without Trousers* – as an abomination and so call for it to be banned and even burned. I know you are proud, and rightly so, of your young democracy, but I see no reason why, if the authorities in France for example can call for works by Voltaire, one of their own countrymen, to be confiscated and destroyed by fire, the same might not happen to works by an Englishman such as I here in the Americas."

Mr Fields did not respond immediately, but paused as if seeking a way round this objection. When he did speak, he clearly felt he had found one. "Charles - hear me out now. I think I have our solution. I think I know the way we must approach this problem."

Mr Dickens offered no response, but waited as Mr Fields continued. "The book needs a good, strong title, as all books do. It needs to be a title your readers will understand and relate to, yet it must also contain the essence of the work, at least in an oblique way, as you have very properly insisted." Mr Dickens making still no response, Mr Fields continued, "Now anyone who is familiar with your work, Charles, will readily admit that some of the most popular and successful amongst them have titles that are the simply name of a lynchpin character - *Barnaby Rudge*, *Oliver Twist*, *David Copperfield*. I am going to suggest that we adopt the same approach here and use the name of a character from the story - but we have to choose the right character and the right name."

"So tell me, James," my master requested, "which character you have in mind."

Mr Fields had his response ready at hand. "I think the choice is obvious - the lad. The cheeky lad who is involved in almost all the action, and whose demise is so expertly portrayed. He has all the characteristics required for a central character - personal strength, strong personality, moral certainty after moments of self-doubt, an element of humour and a high degree of pathos. With a few minor adjustments, this story could easily be made his story with no loss of dramatic impact, and no loss of moral authority. Don't you agree?"

This time, Mr Dickens, after a pause, asked, "And is one of these minor adjustments you are suggesting not having the lad die three quarters of the way through the story? His death is a key plot device, James. Alter that and the story falls apart."

Again, Mr James had his answer ready. "Of course he must die. I wouldn't want him not to die - I think, I hope, you know what I mean by that. The death of the lad is essential. You are right that without his death, the story simply doesn't play out. But he needn't die so soon, need he? He needn't die till the final chapter. He needn't die till the final few pages. Don't you see?"

There was a further pause, a very long pause, before Mr Dickens spoke again. "I can see that your idea has some merit. On the other hand, I have conducted enough revisions to my work in the past to be only too painfully aware that what seems at first a small and simple change can have far reaching and unexpected consequences. In this respect, a writer is like an engineer tending a mighty machine in which every part that moves causes every other part in the machine to move, and he must be on his guard that no part breaks or falls off in the process."

I could feel Mr Field's confidence grow after these statements. "Agreed, Charles, agreed. But will you work with me?"

Still though there was one matter Mr Dickens wanted to see settled. "I cannot give you that agreement, James, till we have a name - a name that suits the character, a name which carries the import of the title we are replacing and will not offend the sensibilities of my American readers. Jacques, or occasionally wee Jacques, as he is named now, hardly fits the bill. Though from the smirk that presently occupies your face, I feel you may already have your suggestion - yes?"

With great enthusiasm, he replied, "Indeed I have, Charles. Indeed I have. We shall call your character and your novel *Trouserless* or, if you will permit, *Trouserless Trouserby.*"

I do not know what response Mr Fields expected from Mr Dickens to this suggestion, but I am willing to suppose that a hollow laugh and the retort *Would you make a laughing stock of me?* would not have been it

"Why a laughing stock?" was Mr Fields' reply. "It is a name that seems to me to have risen straight out of the Charles Dickens canon, if you will forgive my saying so."

"It is a preposterous name," Mr Dickens insisted, "and as a title, it undermines what I hope I am justified in seeing as one of my greater works. I should be accused of self-mockery, self-parody, self-plagiarism, of having run out of ideas."

But Mr Fields was not to be put off. "Charles, my dear fellow, you are an imaginative man, but your vision seems unusually clouded today. Do you think your readers see Pumblechook as a preposterous name? Or Wackford Squeers? Or Dick Swiveller? What about Charity Pecksniff? Even Pickwick himself? I am convinced that young Trouserless Trouserby is waiting even now to join all of these as their fellow."

He was winning Mr Dickens round, for my master then said, "Do you really believe the readers could warm to the death of wee Jacques - Trouserless as you propose to call him - as they did to that of little Nell Trent or young Paul Dombey?"

Fired up now with full, running enthusiasm, Mr Fields said, "Indubitably, Charles. Indubitably. There is not the slightest doubt in my mind. Trouserless will rapidly become another star in the firmament that is the work of Charles Dickens."

I then heard sounds that made me think the men were standing up from their chairs, and my master said, "Then let us shake on it, James. You are the publishing expert after all."

But Mr James had yet one more request to make of Mr Dickens. "And of course we will need to adjust the subtitle of the work as well. Now we have changed your title, calling the work *Trouserless Trouserby: the history of those who, having no trousers, turn against their fellows* seems a little less than plausible. Might I suggest that it become *Trouserless Trouserby : the history of those who, losing hope, turn against their fellows*?" At this, the conversation concluded and all seemed set fair for yet another successful addition to the list of works published under the name Charles Dickens

Our permanent stay in Boston now concluded. Mr Dickens, his wife, myself and the rest of his entourage set out for other centres in America where my master was to speak before audiences drawn from polite society. The cities of New York and Philadelphia, Brooklyn and Baltimore, Washington, Hartford, Providence, Syracuse, Rochester, Buffalo, Albany, Springfield, Worcester, New Haven and New Bedford, and Portland were to make up our itinerary. All seemed to go well. We were welcomed in each new town. Mr Dickens' talks received loud applause and glowing praise. He looked a happy man, as did Mr Fields - until one night, late in the tour, when both he and I were sitting in the foyer of the Steinway Hall in New York at which Mr Dickens was delivering yet another talk. We had both felt that, having heard so many talks already, we might benefit from an evening of relaxation, so we absented ourselves. But it was not to deliver the recreation and repose we hoped for

A boy, wearing one of those very smart uniforms American messengers always have, sought Mr Fields out and handed him a small envelope. Mr Fields rewarded the boy with a coin or two, the young chap saluted, then he turned briskly to walk away. But Mr Fields bade him wait as there may be a reply - from which I deduced that the envelope contained important news for him of a business nature from someone within his publishing house: I have yet to become accustomed to the speed of communication in this country

Whatever was in the message did not please Mr Fields, but his faced visibly turned pale. He dismissed the boy who scurried away. Mr Fields stood up and asked if he might escort me back into the auditorium. He had been called away, he explained, to attend to some urgent affairs, and he was unwilling to leave me alone where I might find myself at the mercy of who knows what or of whom. Naturally I complied. Back in the auditorium, I took up a seat next to Mrs Dickens, close to the podium where her husband was holding forth, and thought little more of what had taken place

Only at breakfast the following morning did explanations begin to emerge, though not before a deeper mystery was revealed. As Mrs Dickens and I went down to the dining room, she told me Mr Dickens was already in conference with Mr Fields in their suite, and she hinted that an angry exchange had begun once they closed the connecting door, though she had no idea what might be the subject of it

Even as we were sitting down to begin our meal, Mr Dickens burst into the dining room and called to his wife. "Catherine, my dear, you must start to pack. Our stay here in the USA has been brought to an abrupt end, I am afraid, and tomorrow we shall be on board ship bound for home. Mr Fields, it seems, has let us down badly, and I can spend no more time in this benighted country than I must. You and your companion," he waved a hand carelessly in my direction. "Yes, you. You must prepare us for departure first thing in the morning. I had the hotel send out a boy to agents and we are booked to sail on the eleven o'clock tide."

So began a day of hurried preparation, without any further word of explanation, for a voyage none of us had expected. Yet all was achieved. All was packed. All was transported to the ship. All was stowed on board or placed in our cabins. And at eleven o'clock in the morning of Wednesday 22nd April, 1868, we were bound for home

Barely had we set sail and left the harbour behind when I saw Mr Dickens standing by the ship's rail, clutching what appeared to be a large box. He seemed a very sorrowful, solitary figure. I went and stood alongside him, though I felt unable to speak. He turned to me and said, "Doubtless you are wanting to hear the reasons for our hurried departure."

I agreed that I was, adding, "I am forced to assume it is connected in some way with the content of the message Mr Fields received whilst we were in the Steinway Hall."

"So you know about that, do you?" he said to me. I explained the circumstances under which I knew. "I take it then that you are still unaware of its ill tidings." Still gazing at the sea, he handed a piece of paper to me and I read it

"Trouserless sales disaster. NY 4 copies. Bos 9. Phil 7. Wash 1. No sales other centres. Advise action."

"I knew I should not have let him talk me into changing the title of the book," Mr Dickens opined. "But even then disaster might have been averted had Mr Fields not come on tour with us. Had he been in his office for the last month, he might have been on hand to talk to the printer's man responsible for the book's cover. That man, I am informed, having no conception of what the words *Trouserless Trouserby* might mean, called at Mr Fields' office where a junior assistant, thinking he was doing something helpful, explained to the man that *trousers* is the world English people use when they want to say 'pants', as the Americans have it. The clerk left the matter at that, thinking it closed

"This printer's man appears unfortunately to have been one of very limited imagination. He took the single word given to him and interpreted it as what the title of the book should really be. This led to many thousands of copies of the book being produced with the single word *PANTS* boldly emblazoned in gold leaf on its cover and on its spine. Because of Mr Fields' absence, no one was on hand to correct the error and so these were the books distributed. As I am sure you may imagine, my American public was left confused. Soon, a rumour circulated that this word was in fact the review of my latest book in the *New York Times*. As one of the more colourful American commentators once put it, *"If they crucify you in the Times, you don't get up and walk away."*

He now lifted the lid of the box he was holding and he took from it a handful of sheets of paper which he held into the wind before letting them go. They flew away from the ship, fluttering slowly down to the sea. A second handful followed. And a third. And more until the box was empty. As he carried out this act, I heard him muttering. "Farewell wee Jacques. Farewell Trouserless Trouserby. Farewell America. And pants to the lot of you."

HELTHE & SAFTYE
The Fake History of Will Shakespeare

I am just a carpenter. Well, I was. My dad trained me up and got me a job helping him. Then, when he died, God rest his soul, the people in charge must have thought I was good enough already because they asked me to take on his job. But I don't work there anymore because a couple of years back, with stars shining in my eyes, I was tempted away

Here is a lesson I have learned: when you're thinking seriously about changing your job, if it should turn out that the man you're going to work for shares the same name as you, just forget about it. Stick where you are because it will not go well. Too many things can go wrong. And that goes double if he is famous enough as well for you already to have heard of him before you meet him. And if you already know what he looks like before you see him - well …

I do wish someone had told me all this before I took this job I now have got

This is the story of how I, Will Shakespeare, a humble artisan, accepted an invitation to come and work for Mr William Shakespeare, poet, playwright, purveyor of written words to His Majesty the King, to the nobility and to the people

Of course, you could say I have only got myself to blame because, if I had not suggested it, the job would never even have existed. I was there the day of the big fire, you see, the day when the old theatre burned down. It was when they set the cannon off. The entire building just went up. Set my bloody pants on fire it did, as well, and all we could find to put them out with was some ale in a jug

Some of the lads have still not forgiven me for that jug of ale. But my pants *were* on fire! Actually on fire, burning with flames, and with me inside them

Anyway, it is because of all that that I told the theatre people they ought to have somebody working for them who would make sure such dangers would never happen, would threat life and limb and property. I suspect it was only when I mentioned the word property that they really started to listen what I had to say

I hadd been at work that morning, you see, fixing up the roof in the charnel house. the one just near to the theatre, as it happens. *Yes. I used to work in the charnel house. Somebody has to*

And that is why my pants were so bloody in the first place and why they burned so easily. They were my work pants, after all. But we were all going together to the theatre in the afternoon, and I just didn't have time to go all the way home to get cleaned up, then get changed, and then come traipsing all the way back again. Not that I had anything to change into anyway. Not that was decent to go about in and was not saved saved for going to church in. So, I just washed my hands a bit, slopped some water on my face, and off we set

Me and the lads were going to see one of those plays about one of the old kings. It was one of the Henrys, I know that much. Most of 'em are Henrys, I think, but don't ask me one which it was 'cos there's been so many and I never was that good with numbers. I do like plays about the olden days though. Lots of running about and shouting. Lots of people getting killed - well, pretending to. They don't really get killed. A real action play. That's what I call a right rollicking good day out

I must say that I'm not all that keen on the soppy love stuff they put in so many of the plays. And especially not on that wit stuff or whatever they call it. That's just talking and being clever, that is. I do not understand any of it. Not a word. Give me a good fight scene

Ho. here's a question I often used to ask. *Is it true that when they put women up on the stage that it's not real women but young lads? And that then they have to get kissed by the real men in the love bits?*

No, no. That is not what I mean ... you know damn well what I mean. Well I never knew the answer to it back then, but I really didn't think it was right. Not then. Now I never bat an eyelid

Fake Histories

Anyway, that remains beside the point. Before we went into the theatre that day, we called in at the little house round the back to get some grub. They know us in there from work. We got some raspberries and some radishes, and we got a fowl. And we got some ale as well, obviously. I would have liked us to get some oysters or scallops or something like that, but it was the end of June and they never seem to sell them in summer. Supposed to be bad for you. Make you puke up or something. *But who are they to tell me what I can and can't eat, eh?* I can remember me saying exactly that

Then we went inside the theatre and tried to pick out a good spot in the pit, somewhere we could see what was happening up on the stage and where we could cast our eyes upon any young women who turned up. Well, you never know. And we wanted a place where we might stand a chance of not getting hit by fruit if the crowd the play turned out not to be to the crowd's liking. Fruit and worse, yeah. And of not getting peed on by the posh folk upstairs

So, the play starts off with some of that clever stuff I said before. Not a good sign, I thought, and it went on like that. To be honest, it didn't seem to be a very good play at all. Even as it got going, I was starting to feel a bit let down, a bit cheated. It was not what had been looking forward to at all and I was getting bored. After a bit, I just grabbed a couple of bones from the fowl. They were still lying where we'd dropped 'em on the ground, and I just picked 'em up and I chucked 'em at the stage. Just like that

That's when these two heavies came and stood near us. They were big blokes – *seriously big* blokes - with shaven heads. And all in black - black jerkins, black hose, heavy black boots - and they all wore the same armband. Me and the lads, well, we just looked at each other. We didn't know for sure they were working for the theatre, but the armbands made it a pretty safe bet. They'd all got the same picture on them. It was a bloke's face. You know the one, the famous one with the bald head and the pointy beard

We all know that face, don't we? You see it on the ale-houses, and even more so inside the ale-houses on the ale casks

Even if we don't know his name, we all know his face. Of course, it's only since then that I've found out that people actually pay him to let his face be seen in places like the ale-houses. Did you know that? After the king, he's probably the only face folk can all recognise. And we all know it to be the face of the bloke who makes all the plays up, which I imagine must be why the theatre heavies had it on their arms. But I never knew what his name was, not back then. I do now, of course, and I know you do, but does anybody else?

So, these big blokes just stood there and - well – they loomed. But I don't think it was just us they were looking at. I think the whole crowd was starting to get a bit narky. People want something to be happening up on the stage and they weren't getting it. They were shuffling their feet. They were starting to talk. And I'm sure that, here and there, there were couples who were – you know - at it. Doing it like couples do. The old beast with two backs. You do know. I mean, most of us do save it for somewhere a bit more private. At least outside

But then it happened. You might say the earth moved, sort of thing. What it really was was the loudest noise I have ever heard, a dirty great explosion. First my ears rang, and then I thought I had gone deaf. What they'd done was let off a cannon on the stage. I think it was supposed to be as part of a celebration they were meant to be showing for the birth of the old queen, the one who's dead now, 'cos the play was the one about her dad. I'd worked that much out. He's a long time dead, but he was one of the Henrys, wasn't he? The cannon was only a part of the story, I think, but whatever it was, it had gone wrong. I had gone really wrong

The big blokes scrammed. They just set off. I thought they'd got scared, but later on I saw they were making sure all the players got out of the place safe, pushing the paying audience out of the way whenever they had to

Fire was catching hold of more and more bits of the theatre. It started in the straw in the roof and fell down on everyone. And of course, people were making a rush for the doors trying to get outside, though some of us at least were trying to put the fire out. But it seemed that was not working

Now straightaway it struck me as a bit stupid that there was nothing on the stage or anywhere else for that matter that could be just grabbed and used to put a fire out, like some pails of water or dirt or something. I know the players would have to be able to move about round them, but that would be easy enough to sort out. You could make the pails a really bright colour, bright red or bright yellow or something, and put them somewhere everyone could see them

I was having these thoughts, but I was still trying to stamp on the flames to put them out

And they have to practice the play before they do it, don't they? So everybody knows what to say and where to stand and that. What's that thing they call it? Rehearsal? They can rehearse what to do with the pails, and how to put a fire out. This is just how I used think in those days. And they need to think a lot more about how to organise getting people out of the theatre because that was something else that did not work properly. People were pushing each other and getting in each other's way. And like I said, the big blokes were getting in everybody's way as they took the players outside. In fact, looking back, it comes as a surprise that no one got seriously hurt that night. But no one did – no one except for me and my pants

When we did finally get outside, when we had decided we were all fighting a losing battle against the fire, I expected to see mayhem, but actually there was nothing of the sort

There was a big group of people who had formed a human chain bringing pails of water up from the river, trying to put the fire out, but as well as that there was about a dozen people, mostly men but a few women with them, in a group of their own

I'm sure they hadn't been there when we went in, but they were there now. They'd all got black jerkins on a bit like the ones the heavies were wearing, except these had no armbands, but they did have a red crest over their left breast. I don't know where they came from, but they were there and they were busy. All of them had scrolls and quills, and they were getting people to line up, whilst they walked up and down to find out who'd got burns, and who'd got grazes and cuts, and who'd got clothing that was burnt or torn. Very quickly people started calling this the *help line*, but as far as I could see there was precious little help to be had. The scribes were just writing down people's names and making lists of all the things they'd supposedly lost or had damaged, and all the injuries they'd supposedly suffered. Listening to it all, I have to say I was starting to get a bit angry. The stories people we're telling! And the scribes just wrote it all down

There was me: I had been the one with my pants on fire. Yet there was all these rogues, these scullions, who just got out of the way as fast as they could, and they were claiming that they all had had accidents that were not their fault, and that they had all been out in the last few days and bought the clothes they were wearing. But you could see it was mostly just the same sort of patched-up old stuff like we all have

The scribes though, without actually saying as much, were letting them all think the theatre people would just dish out handfuls of silver. To say sorry, I suppose. But what for? Why people believed it, I don't know. But some people will believe anything, won't they?

That was when I spotted him - the man, the baldy, pointy-bearded man - just in front of where I work. He was looking harassed to say the very least, and that did not didn't surprise me. I thought I might go and share my ideas with him, but there were lots of people around him, and they were all angry. That is the disadvantage of having the second most famous face in the kingdom, I suppose

I changed my approach: I nipped in just behind the crowd and waited for the right moment, just as he got close to the charnel house door. Then I reached out and grabbed him, opened the door and dragged him through. And I slammed the door fast and threw the bolt. There was a lot of banging on the door from outside. But it's a big, strong and sturdy door. They weren't going to get through that very quickly

I think he realised that he had just had a lucky escape, and he leaned against the wall and muttered to himself. Then he looked at me and suddenly a shadow passed across his face

It dawned on me he must be thinking I had only dragged him in here to get to the front of the revenge queue and give him a bit of a kicking. So I told him that was far from my aim, told him about the scribes lining people up to make claims against the theatre, against him

He rolled his eyes and began muttering again

I decided that, now I had this chance, it just had to be taken, so I started reeling off all the ideas I had had since the fire started, and all the different things we'd wanted and had not had to try and put it out with. I also told him how I thought it was criminal that the bodyguards had pushed people out of the way to make sure the players all got to safety before anyone else. I told him that he was his own worst enemy, that he would only have himself to blame if people did turn up demanding handfuls of silver from him. I really have no idea where I got my words from, but, with what must have been a rush of blood to my head, I told him this:

'Thou giv'st thy players all that wit to spout.
'Far better that they have their wits about
'Them as they promenade across thy stage,
'All present hazards thereupon to gauge.
'What if on thy very stage some waif be
'Injured through this lack of helthe and saftye?'

Well that shook him. It did. To be honest, it shook me a bit too, but it really stopped him in his tracks, for a moment. Then he started complaining I was wrong if I took him for a fool who knew not how to run his affairs, so I had another go:

'What know'st thou, sir, of who would be a fool,
'If thou refused to make it be a rule
'That plays, when they're presented in that place,
'Must not throw dangers in the people's face?
'Consider well how thou would'st soon be named
'By those who through thy negligence were maimed.'

At last - finally - I had his attention. From the frown he had been wearing grew a smile, a big smile, on his old and baldy, beardy face. It was a smile that seemed to have had an idea, a solution to some problem

Through his smile, he asked me if I felt I had the skills to make these things I said come true, if I had the vision to make a safer place for putting on his plays. I just nodded, then explained all I had been thinking

At length, when I had finished and after he had slapped me on the back, his arm was round my shoulder, it was as if we were the best of lifelong friends. He licked his lips and jerked his head ever so slightly. He wanted us to go somewhere. Was he asking me - telling me - to go with him to the tavern?

We set off. We used a different door to get out of the charnel house, one well away from the crowd that was so eager to meet him

We paused to look back at the theatre. It must have been as dry as tinder for it had all but burned away and the flames were subsiding. A crowd was around it still, and I could see my mates were still among them. With pails in their hands, they had been trying to save the place but they now just stood and watched, knowing there was little more to do but stop it spreading if it did flare up again

I did think my new companion and I might go to join them, but no. And we also passed *The Swan*, the tavern on the corner by the theatre. Rightly so, I think, for a different crowd was gathered outside there, an all together uglier crowd who cared little for helping the situation, it seemed to me. They seemed only to care for drinking and making an awful noise, and perhaps for seeking someone to blame for all that had happened. Our arrival could well have started a riot, though the tavern keeper must be doing well enough out of it all

Of course, baldy man was not going to admit anything like that. He had to insist we had passed the tavern only as I smelled so foul of ale already that I needed no more. I told him I smelled only so foul of ale as ale was all we had to put my pants out with when they caught fire in his theatre, thus showing all I had earlier told him to be true. He just smirked, tapped the side of his nose and bade me follow

We went not to a tavern at all but to a different place just around the corner. Not a tavern, this, but very like one, it seemed to me. It has a sign above its door that shows a woman's head with tails like fishes' tails, unless they are supposed to be braids, but they look like fish to me. *Is this what a mermaid looks like?* I remember wondering

I had never been to this place before, though I had heard many speak of it. Here they sell that new-fangled stuff all the players and all the aristocratic ladies love so much, as some say. Others say it is an abomination, a heathenish brew. Most just call it coffee. I found it foul smelling stuff that looks like mud and tastes no better. I didn't partake, though my host seemed like he could drink the place dry of it

After a time though, he gave me leave to speak and tell him what improvements I felt that I, a mere artisan as he called me, could make to the conduct of productions in the theatre he and his company had built from nothing

Again I don't know why or how, but I responded quickly in the style it now seems I had learned from his plays:

'Not from nothing, sir, for I've heard say
'Thy men work'd timbers they did take away
'From where another house had early been.
'Didst thou not there put plays on for the Queen?
'I've heard that to that site the people swarmed.
'Is this not so? Am I yet ill-informed?'

I'd barely got the words out when he forced his hand across my mouth. This tale is one he has no desire for him to hear or me to tell, I thought to myself. I supposed thereby it must be true, as I had heard, that The Globe Theatre, now burned to the ground, had consisted mainly of timbers that a troupe of players had stolen from an earlier theatre that they had often played in, one north of our great river

His face turned stern as he took another sip from his brown drink, and I know not how our meeting might have developed from there had not, at that precise moment, a group of men burst into the building looking for my companion. And glad they were to see him. The clamour outside the theatre, they said, was growing, even as the flames had died, leaving only the foul reek of smoke and glow of embers. People, egged on and provoked by the scribes I had seen, were crying out for payment. But the building, they reported, was lost entirely

Then he looked back at me, smiled again broader than ever, looked back to his friends and boldly declared I was to be their answer - much to the surprise of his friends, who looked me up and down. They seemed less than impressed. He told them in the briefest form that I was a man of ideas, a man they all needed to know, then leaped directly to his feet whilst I still reeled at his description. He called out to the keeper of the house that payment would be made on his return, and set off, leading us all out into the street and back towards the theatre. Though I am sure the keeper of the house would have preferred his payment there and then, he made no attempt to stop us leaving

I must declare how I do admire these players. They look at situations and take them on far braver than an ordinary man

As we approached the theatre site, still smouldering, still smoking, but all flames died away, and all but the sturdiest timbers tumbled to the ground in ashes, my instinct was to slow down and seek a place to hide from the crowd who all were aflame for the baldy man's blood. But not he. Boldly he strode through the crowd, easily waving away all cries for him to stop, dragging me with him as he went. With his finger held high in the air, he headed direct for a cart that stood outside what remained of the main way into the theatre and hauled himself, and me, on to it. As I stood by, I watched him turn to face the mob, and I could swear he grew taller by a foot, so what he looked like to all the folk below I barely can imagine even now

Before he even spoke, the crowd fell silent. And all he did was look at them. Slowly he turned his head and looked at them, at every single one of them. And every single one of them knew he had looked directly at them. And then he spoke to them. He spoke to all, but as with the look he spoke to each one. He told them only things that they already knew - that the theatre now was destroyed and in ruins, that they all must now be feeling shocked, that they all must now have suffered much that day. But he told this to each one and somehow not to all, so much that, when he went on to say some unscrupulous, uncaring souls who obviously had suffered less than they or he - or even not at all, he added most pointedly - were seeking to exploit the day and extort funds that truly weren't their due, I felt the crowd become firm in its resolve that none should take advantage of this honest man – this honest, working man - who'd suffered more than any. He had lost his world, it seemed. He had lost his Globe. And then he beckoned me and bade me come stand by him as he spoke, and he whispered in my ear to tell him my name

I whispered back, "*Will, sir. Will Shakespeare.*"

And he glared hard into my eyes. *'Mock me with my own name?'* was how he responded to me. I will admit it took me quite a time, till long after we had left the site, to work out just what he meant by that. And when I did, it made me think no better of him

At that time not a little scared, I nonetheless replied, quietly, just to him:

'What's in a name? That which we call a pig
'By any other name would smell as rank …'

He hushed me, and spoke through gritted teeth, *'And mock me with a travesty of my own words.'* Then he turned again to face the crowd, and again they stilled to hear his words

He pulled me forward, to the edge of the cart - so close to the edge I feared I might stumble and fall off, or he might push and cause me to tumble. But his aim quickly became clear

He wanted to show me to the crowd, to tell them that I had all the ideas that, after he had rebuilt his Globe, would make sure no one ever suffered such a dire fate again as had been seen this day

He told them he had only left the theatre to seek me out and make sure my expertise would be available to all of them when they came to see the plays he would once again present in his rebuilt Globe:

'My friends, look well upon this happy soul.
'He'll lead us on from here unto our goal
'To make anew a stage where all ends well,
'Where fancies come alive, where tales we tell
'Will make you laugh and cry, but never more
'Send people running, screaming, to the door.'

He told them I had been appointed to a special new role that would be for the benefit of the nation, of the people, even of his majesty the king himself. He told them that from this day forth I was to be known as Gentleman Responsible for the Helthe and the Saftye of the Person of His Majestye the King in All His Palaces and Courts. My jaw dropped

Yet the change that came about was astounding. Minutes before, all had been baying for his money and even for his head: now they cheered him, they cheered me. They cheered everybody and everything - except the scribes. The scribes with their lists of names simply slunk away. They knew they had lost the day

Below us, I could see his fellows. They were looking up at us. They were cheering and applauding, and grinning fit to split their faces. To me it seemed they were egging their colleague on for they fully knew what was in his mind. All the while, I wished that I could know the same, for I knew that I was in his mind and I had this desperate feeling that he was about to make some major new demand of me

Of course he is, I thought. *Why else has he dragged me up here and shown me to the crowd?*

But he went and stood behind me, whispering in my ear to tell them all that I had told him in the *starburk*. I told him I didn't know what a *starburk* was. So, he told me it was the coffee place, and I said I couldn't talk to all this crowd and tried to turn to look at his face, but he held my arm firm. Truly it felt like he meant to hurt me. I know I opened my mouth but I heard not a word come out of it

Again, he whispered to me, laughing that in front of people I had lost all the eloquence I had earlier shown when none but he was present. I was trying to retreat, but he whispered I was to stand my ground. He whispered most insistently I was to repeat all that he would tell me to say, so I made to begin

At least I tried, but even I couldn't hear myself, so the crowd had not a chance. Then I felt my arm twist just a little more, and I tried again, and with relief I found a voice this time, and I spoke the words his voice gave to mine

'Today we've seen a place consum'd in fire,
'A place that once did burn with all desire
'And hate and love and scorn and battle cries.
'But now in ruin and in ash it lies.
'Another theatre soon you all will see
'With all the former's pomp and majesty.'

Loud cheering began. For sure it had begun with Mr Shakespeare's three associates, but quickly it ran through the crowd, and they began to clap, and to throw hats and many other strange and various things into the air

At last Mr Shakespeare let my arm free and turned me to face him, my back now to the cheering crowd. He raised his arms, as I thought to embrace me in celebration at what we had just achieved, but no! He pushed me, full in the chest, and caused me to fall. Fall backwards. Fall backwards off the cart and plummet towards the ground, whilst he laughed and cheered like the crowd

Not for the first time on this strangest of strange days, the natural course as I perceived it failed to be the case. I did not hit the ground. I hit what proved to be the upturned hands of the cheering crowd. The broke my fall, held me safe, passed me above their heads, like a piece of driftwood floating aimlessly on the surface of the river

When I recovered from my shock - and from what so nearly had been an ungovernable urge to empty my bowels - it became a strangely pleasant feeling. I saw the sky above me with its white and fluffy summer clouds, and I felt almost as though I was floating with them, almost as though I might reach and touch them and be a part of the heavens

This was it. This was the moment - the moment when I knew I had to be part of this world that makes the dreams and shows the action to the world. I had watched it so many times from the pit and now I could be one of the dream-makers. It was the most exciting feeling I had ever known

How long the feeling lasted, how long I was this strange part of the crowd, I cannot know. Soon enough though, I washed up back at the cart where I had started. Mr Shakespeare himself pulled me back from the crowd and on to the cart. I was still fulfilling a purpose for him even now, and once again he addressed the crowd as one who is born to the task which I truly believe he is

He made me take a bow, at which again I nearly fell from the cart: *we'll need a rail here if people are to work like this again*, I told myself, whilst Mr Shakespeare was telling the crowd my name. The *responsible gentleman*, he called me, *William Shakespeare, Officer of Helthe & Saftye*, laughing that I shared my name with him, assuring them I was not his son

If he had some of my blood, he joked - I hope he joked, *then he would not be so ugly*

And that is how it all began - my new job, my new career, my new life and all my new woes. Yes, woes. For a life in the theatre is not all roses thrown on the stage and applause and free mugs of ale in *The Swan*

It took barely a year for the replacement theatre to be drawn up and built and, I believe, paid for in full, not built with materials spirited away in darkness as its earlier form had been. Though I confess I know nothing of how the money was obtained, these players are not the fools so many in the ordinary world suppose

I, of course, had my own job to do and was given all freedom to carry it out. I got my bright red pails in all important places to help put out fires if they occurred: sand drawn from the river and dried we found to be a far more fit material than water or dirt. With help from a local churchman, we found a supply of green stained glass, and used it to fashion sconces that would hold sturdy candles which we lit at each performance: in this way we showed folk where lay the ways out of the building. After some resistance, I even persuaded them that a corner be provided at each end of the gallery where men might go and pee in peace, if they be minded, saving the poor wretches below from needless, foul-odoured soakings. Some raised the thought that something of the kind be provided for women as well, but I firmly pointed out that no decent woman would so disgrace herself in a public place, and all were in agreement with my thought. The theatre must become a decent place, we all concurred, with such encouragements to impropriety and lewdness avoided at all cost

Yet with each new production, with every single performance in our new theatre, would come queues of people, players and artisans alike, demanding work of me

Had I watched their movements on the stage and made sure they would not trip or fall at any point? Was there no way I could ensure they wouldn't slip when clearing fake blood and guts up from the stage? Was I sure their costumes wouldn't catch or chafe? Was I sure the stains used to create our backdrops would not bring a rash to the hands? Could I be sure their swords were safe and no one would be hurt in fight scenes?

Those history plays I'd so enjoyed when I was but a carpenter from round the corner have now become something for me to dread. Whatever we make the swords from, no matter how well we rehearse the fights, some careless player may easily have someone's eye out. Anyone who does not look where he is going can slip or trip on anything. Every time a player runs across the stage, he can stumble over his own feet, and if he falls with his head upon something hard, like a bright red pail filled with sand for example, it will hurt or even bleed. I can no more prevent these things than change the weather

Some scenes I dread above most others, no matter what measures we take to keep the players safe - like when they fall upon Coriolanus or upon Julius Caesar, or on any other unfortunate who is murdered violently in the course of the play. We put thick woollen vests under the robes, but it fools only those who are weak in the eyes - or in the head. And still it doesn't stop the players coming back at me afterwards to complain all over again.

And that Titus Andronicus - well - I never want to get involved in that one again

I've noticed also some of those scribes, the ones with the scrolls and quills who turned up after the fire, now hanging round outside our new theatre, and in *The Swan,* and in that *starburk* place. Though I have learned, by the way, that coffee does not taste anything like mud, not when you get used to it. In fact, I have grown to love it, and spend a good deal of my time - and my money - there. And the sign above the door is a mermaid, or so the man who keeps the place insists

But I know what the scribes are up to. They are planting fears in the minds of the players, and of everyone else who works here, that The Globe is not a safe place for them to work

They send people to me just to ask stupid questions

Will Juliet be safe when he leans out over that balcony?

Is Nick Bottom sure he's not breathing in stuff that might make him choke when he's being the wall?

Stupid questions

Juliet is always told, whichever of our boys plays the part, not to lean too far out and that, if he does, whatever happens to him will be his own silly fault. Nick Bottom's wall isn't even a real wall, and the only thing he could breathe in to do him any harm would be the breath and the stink of his fellow players: well truly I'm not being made responsible for that

But players are a superstitious bunch, and the artisans are by and large easily led. Not only do they take in all these ideas, but they have ideas of their own that are just as daft

Players and artisans alike all go weak at the knee and in the head if anyone should whistle in the theatre. Now I grew up a working man and whistling is sometimes the only thing you can do to attract your fellows' attention, especially when there is sawing and hammering and all the sounds of real work going on. Then there is that name that none will say (I won't use it here in case they see it, or hear about it, and it sets them all a-twitter!): it may all be very well to say it if you are doing the play it appears in, so I am told, but you must not say it at any other time. I must not say it even when Mr Shakespeare himself needs to instruct me in what each new production requires of me. Even he who wrote the play must not be heard to say it, on pain of who knows what

But the daftest one of all, or so I believe, is the one about the ghosts. So the players say, a theatre should be left empty and silent for one day in every week, and with a light burning, mark you, to appease the ghosts. And the light must burn free, not be guarded by glass or a gauze or anything

When I ask what ghosts, I am decried. How easily they all forget that I have been associated with this building since before it grew from the ashes of its older self. They forget that the only reason this new theatre was built at all is because the old one was burned to the ground. And most of all they forget that the only thing ever to have met its end here in all that time was a pair of my pants. Now if they're afraid of the ghost of my pants …

Fake Histories

But I could probably live with all of that if it were not for the worst thing of all, the thing I can do nothing to change - my own blessed name. If I were not the young Will Shakespeare, I'm sure these players all would soon forget that I didn't grow up in what they call *the business*. I'm sure they all would assume I was just a journeyman like they, keen to make the working day go well and live as comfortably as I might off the meagre wage they pay, just as they all do

But even the boss makes it no easier for me. Whenever Mr Shakespeare is around, he makes a point of calling me Young Will and ruffling my hair whenever he finds me seated: he cannot reach it whenever I stand

Well this is what I think of all of them, and if they don't like it, I'm sure I can go back to the charnel house

'Correctitude of politic be damned.
'I wouldn't want to be there if they hammed
'Their way through life just as they do on stage.
'Their actions oft'times put me in a rage.
'They're such a bunch of fops and Fancy Dans.
'This business of the show? I wash my hands.'

No. Of course I don't mean it. The fake blood is much easier to clean off than the real stuff you get when the sheep and goats and pigs and cows are being slaughtered. The smell of the grease paint is far, far better than the smell of rotting offal and all the other foul things they pull out of the gut of a beast

I just have to sound off sometimes and do things like this from time to time to remind Mr William Shakespeare that I'm a Shakespeare too - Will Shakespeare, Helthe & Saftye Officer

VALENTINE'S DAY
The Fake History of a Hit

Morning is the time when the city is at its most demanding, when the streets are full of movement and of people. But the city is arrogant. The city cares nothing for people. Even the crowd cares for nothing but its own selfish need to be somewhere else. A man meanwhile can lose himself in the city, in the crowd. A man can hide in plain sight, can throw the seekers off the scent, can run in the city and not leave a trace

It's 9.00 AM. It's February. It's Chicago. And it's cold. It's a day when things that go down in the city can take down men in the city - big men - and lay them low. The city will not care. The city will go on about its business like nothing has happened, like it always does. But the people will know – some of them will

The place has been set - the SMC Cartage warehouse at 2122 North Clark Street, Lincoln Park on the Northside. The time has been set - 10.30 in the AM. The target has been set - Mr Adelard Cunin: not the name most people know him by, but the name his folks gave him when he was born back in '93 in Minnesota, his real name. The world, the papers, history too - all have come to know him as Bugs Moran, leader of the Northside gang and only real rival to Al Capone's Southside dominance. The weapons have been chosen, but this is not going to be like some old-time duel in a kid's storybook adventure because the chosen weapons are Thompson sub-machine guns, and only one side will have them

A lot of preparation has gone into this hit. A lot of plans have been made. A lot of moves have been rehearsed. A lot of palms have been greased. Gunther Keller has his role. But he has no need to be in place for almost an hour, so he goes off to get himself a cup of coffee. There is a place he knows on North Lincoln Avenue, a few streets over from North Clark, where they serve the best coffee along with something they call dry cooked rolled oats with cream. It's like porridge, but you need a knife and a fork to eat it. Gunther loves the stuff

Gunther also loves Martha. Martha is this cute little lady who works in the place, the one with the curly hair that's not quite blonde but certainly not anything else. She's the one who usually serves him his coffee and his dry cooked rolled oats. And she wipes the tables and mops the floor. Gunther fell in love with Martha the moment first he saw her here in the coffee shop, and he keeps going back again, and again, just to see her. Martha doesn't love Gunther. At least he doesn't think she does. In fact, Gunther doesn't know for sure if Martha has ever even noticed him except to wipe his table or serve him his breakfast. But she may have and, he figures, a guy can dream, can't he? She may notice him one day – one day when he makes his name. She may notice him today, because today may be the day when he makes his name

But right now, Gunther is losing himself in the city, in the crowd. He is hiding in plain sight. There are no seekers yet, no scent to follow. But he is running in the city and leaving not a trace. He's just this guy after all. Sometimes he takes breakfast here, but no one notices if he doesn't

After his breakfast, which includes two cups of coffee today, but still not a flicker of acknowledgement from Martha, he sets out. He is going to be in place with ten maybe twenty minutes to spare. He pulls down his hat, lifts his coat collar, adjusts his muffler. It really is very cold out here

On the way back to North Clark Street, he passes a flower store. Suddenly, the significance of the day dawns on him. "It's Valentine's Day." He can't say for sure whether he spoke these words or simply thought them, but he backtracks and goes inside. "Can I buy a single red rose?" he asks. "To give to a lady?" He has already worked out that carrying a whole bunch of roses, or of anything else, would probably not be a good idea. Not today

"Sure you can," the flower girl tells him. "You want me to wrap it?"

"Wrap it?" He has never bought flowers before and can't picture what wrapping one might look like

Seeing his confusion, the flower girl demonstrates. "Watch. I fold this piece of paper over like so, then roll it. Make it look like a cone, see? Then I slide the rose inside so it's less likely to get beaten up as you carry it to the lady in your heart. Whadd'ya think?"

"Why that's swell, miss." He really is impressed by the simplicity. "But there's one thing. Can you make it smaller?"

"Smaller?"

"Shorter. Cut off some of the stem? You see I need to carry it in my pocket, the one inside my coat, here." Seeing the flower girl knit her brows, he adds, "I have some - ah - business to attend to first and it just wouldn't be the right thing to be seen carrying a flower with me. You know what business people can be like."

The flower girl well aware of what business this young man is likely to be associated with, but she is happy to oblige. He slides Martha's gift gently into place in the pocket of his overcoat, carefully arranging his billfold and his pens and his comb so they might help save it from being crushed. Today for sure will be the day Martha notices him: his mind is made up on that

Finally back at North Clark, he goes straight into the rooming house across the street from 2122, and upstairs to the room where he meets up with Phil and Harry, the Keywell brothers. They are members of Detroit's Purple Gang, in Chicago posing as cabbage farmers from Cicero as far as the authorities are concerned, though the

Northside gang members converging on the warehouse expect them to be bringing a liquor shipment supposedly paid for by Capone's Southsiders. Any blow Moran's boys can land on Capone's mob is a welcome blow, another small success in the long and bitter street war being waged between rival gangs

In fact, the Keywells have the warehouse under close surveillance and will go no closer to it than they now are. They confirm to Gunther that several members of the Northside gang have already turned up and are inside, but so far as they can tell, Moran has not yet shown his handsome Irish face. This is why Gunther is here. He knows Moran well enough to be able to recognise him in the street, through the rooming house window, from the other side of the street. He doesn't flatter himself: he doesn't see this as some kind of honour, not a feather in his cap. He knows he got the job because his low status in the mob makes him expendable. If it were all to go wrong, Gunther Keller would be the one who wound up feeding the fish in Lake Michigan, a comfortable pair of concrete overshoes protecting his feet from the cold water

Gunther lights a cigarette, stubs it out immediately, then puts it back between his lips. This is what he will use to make his signal. At 10.25 precisely, he will leave the building again, walk across the road towards the warehouse, then head off back up town. As he crosses the road, he will discard his cigarette. Throwing it to his left means Moran is in the warehouse and the strike should begin. To his right means no Moran and no hit. He checks his watch. 10.03. Twenty-two minutes. Twenty-two minutes could turn into a long time. He could have had another cup of coffee. He could have spent a few more minutes looking at Martha

Nineteen minutes. It occurs to him he might talk to the Keywells. But he doesn't know them. Doesn't know a single thing about them. He does know enough people who, for the wrong word in the wrong ear on the wrong day, have wound up with lead between the eyes. Who needs to talk, he thinks?

Thirteen minutes. His right hand pulls at the left lapel of his overcoat and he peers inside. As he checks that the rose is still intact, he also checks the suspicious looks on the Keywells' mugs. Both have turned to see what he is doing. He risks a smile, and a few words. "A present for my girl," he tells them as he shows them the rose. "For Valentine's Day. Just making sure it's still in one piece."

First one then the other Keywell smile back at him. "The ladies, eh?" one of the brothers says. "What we go through for them." The rose is returned carefully to its place

Nine minutes. He stands up and peers through the window from behind the Keywells. Just people. Just the crowd, all needing to be somewhere else

Four minutes. He thinks about lighting the cigarette and smoking it, but thinks again. He'd be sure to stub it out and have no time to light another. Then, just as Gunther is realising that these thoughts make no sense, a Keywell says, "There."

Fake Histories

There, emerging from a car and headed to the warehouse is a figure - from the height, the build, the stylish, expensive looking coat and the pale fedora, Bugs Moran. None of them can see his face, but a coat like that? It must be Moran. Three minutes

He checks he has the cigarette. It still between his lips. Then he heads from the room out into the corridor. He says nothing to the Keywells by way of parting remark, and they say nothing back to him. They just watch him leave, then turn to observe the scene that is set to unfold

At the front door of the rooming house, before opening it, he checks his watch again. A minute left, just over. He feels nervous. All he must do is walk through the street door, cross the road and throw the cigarette away. And he feels nervous. He feels more nervous than he can recall ever having felt before. He must throw the cigarette to the left. To the left? Yes - to the left means Moran is in the warehouse and the strike should begin

The last few seconds tick down on his watch - and he throws open the street door, waits for a truck to pass then sets out across the road. Halfway across, he takes the cigarette from between his lips, holds it between the front of his thumb and the nail of his middle finger, and flicks it as far as it will go. It flies in an arc, not hitting any passer-by or passing vehicle, and Gunther Keller veers off to the left, his work here done, heading for the coffee shop and for Martha. Today is the day she is going to notice him - he is very confident

As he strides almost without a care through the streets, he falters only very slightly at a sound that pricks up the ears of everyone around him. A sound all too common in Chicago - the sound of gunfire. Rapid gun fire. Machine gun fire

He sets off again, smiling as he almost swaggers into the coffee shop. He glances round looking for Martha, but he doesn't see her. He does see a table by the window, so walks across and sits down there. He takes off his hat and places it on the far side of the table. Very carefully he takes the rose from his pocket. The paper wrapper has been flattened just a little from the round shape the flower girl made, but the flower inside is still intact, still a beautiful red rose. He places it on the near side of the table, immediately in front of him

He looks round again and this time sees a face he recognises, a face he really does not want to see, not here and not now. He sees a well-known street thug called Ted Newberry, a big noise on the Northside, and now, in his later years, thought by many to be a top advisor to Bugs Moran. Newberry sees Gunther, recognises him - and he indicates so to the person sharing the table with him. Gunther can only see this person's back but he is chilled when he recognises - from the height, the build, the stylish, expensive looking coat and the pale fedora - Bugs Moran

"This cannot be," Gunther is thinking. But it is. If Moran is here now, then the man he saw walking into the SMC Cartage warehouse at 2122 North Clark Street, Lincoln Park was certainly not Moran. Gunther knows that he has unleashed the fury and the firepower of the Southside against the wrong man. "This cannot be," he is still thinking. But he knows it is. He know it cannot be other

Already the Northside will be looking to take him out: already they were well before today: he is a known Southsider after all. But soon his own Southside buddies will be after him too, after him to punish this failure. No longer can Gunther hide in plain sight. No longer can he throw the seekers off the scent. No longer can he run in the city and not leave a trace. Sooner or later – probably sooner – the city will offer him up to one or other of his enemies: and everybody was his enemy now

Moran and Newberry stand. They turn to walk towards the coffee shop door, a walk that will take them straight by Gunther's table. Gunther knows he has nowhere to run, no time to run, so he simply remains static in his chair staring intently at the red rose in front of him. Moran saunters straight by and out through the door. But Newberry pauses

Gunther tries to ignore him, but Newberry pulls out the other chair, sits down opposite, faces him and addresses him directly. "It's been a long time, Keller. We don't seem to mix in the same circles no more," and after a long pause, "You got nothing to say for yourself?"

Unable to think of a response that would do the occasion justice, Gunther just keeps on staring at Newberry. Newberry leans forward and whispers more or less in Gunter's ear. "We know what you had planned for today. We know where you planned to do it. And we heard the shooters." Newberry glares straight into Gunther's eyes. Gunther stares past him. "Lucky for us we knew, or you Southside wops might've done some damage. Not just knock off a few wops who turned up there in return for a couple of bottles of hooch. And you want to know the up side? We're going to get most of those bottles back now – thanks to you, Keller. Thanks to you

"And it's lucky too for us that we knew you would be back here to make cow-eyes at curlilocks over there. So whilst I really would like to wish you congratulations on carrying out your part in the plan so well, my sadness is that you will not now live to enjoy your success."

Newberry stands up, very abruptly. And only one thought is left now for Gunther Keller - pain - pain – intense pain. Faster than can be imagined, Newberry produces a blade – narrow and sharp, so sharp - and slashes Gunther's throat deeply and smoothly and completely

Gunther goes into shock, unable to move or speak or do anything. Newberry goes into high gear. After dropping the blade, a barbershop razor, he is outside the coffee shop in a second, almost knocking Martha off her feet as he passes

Martha has seen that young man arrive, that nice-looking young man who likes so much the dry cooked rolled oats, always with cream, and coffee of course. She had seen him and served him when he was in earlier in the day, and is surprised to see him back again so soon. Pleasantly surprised. Always he looks as though he is trying to be brave enough to talk to her. She wishes he would, but he never seems able. She respects that. And she feels foolish that she is just too bashful to encourage him

She approaches the young man's table from behind and, as she does so, has the oddest sensation that something is not right. On the table, in front of the young man, she sees something red. Not a red rose, not the red rose that now lays unseen on the floor beneath the table where it fell during the act of extreme violence that has just taken place. What she sees is red and liquid and moving - almost boiling. Something like - blood. Blood

Martha screams. And the city goes on about its business like nothing has happened, like it always does

DEMON AGREEMENT
The Fake History of Fake Histories

He turned his key in the lock, dropped the latch, headed straight for the kitchen. After pulling down the blind, he put the kettle on: only a cup of tea – good, strong tea - would be enough in this circumstance. He flicked on the light. It was sunny and bright outside, but he needed some serious privacy – did not want anyone staring in, did not want to be disturbed by anybody. He had lately had far too little privacy. Somehow suddenly he had moved from having a public profile to being public property, and that was not a good feeling. The media can do that to you

Yet it had started off so well. When he first self-published his book about a decade ago, after the slow start, and after the big stunt, things had really happened. So maybe slagging off the leader of the free world was a bit of a cheap shot, but that particular POTUS had been such a mug that he had deserved it. There had been a bit of serious help deployed, as well, but once he had offended the president, everyone wanted to know him. The reviews, the news sites, the podcasts had described the stunt as *'courageous'*, *'brave'*, *'heroic'*. He knew different. He knew it had just been a stunt. A cheap stunt at that. Cheap in one sense, at least

Nevertheless, though only a slim volume, *Fake Histories* did whatever passed for flying off the shelves back in those online-purchase-driven days. Could a book fly off the screen? Could it download like cats and dogs? *Come one, world*, he had thought. *We need someone making up some modern clichés here*

Fake Histories made its mark on the world. *Today's fake news is tomorrow's fake history*, he had explained in the book's subtitle, but there was nothing fake about what had happened to him in the decade since. He had gone, in quick succession, from skint to mint, from back street to front page, from no-go to hit show. Once he had dismissed himself as a sad, skint, selfish, stupid, fat, ugly, bald, old loner. Suddenly, seemingly from nowhere, there was a queue of interesting, intelligent, attractive women eager to show him just how much they did not agree with that assessment. And even a couple of men, too, though he passed on them. And the web news loved it. They celebrated his life and his lifestyle. It had been an entertaining and an exhausting time, and mercifully brief

Brief only because, very soon after it started, he had met the One. She had walked into a book signing looking almost unconcerned – almost – and looking exactly like the One, like the one he had always imagined and given up all hope of finding. She had it all. She had the hair - almost but not quite shoulder length, auburn and with the slightest hint of a wave. She had the height – five feet six and three quarters, not a sliver more. She had the voice – she was a trained singer, as it happened. She had the grace – and dancer too. And she had the smile – electric, like shadows receding and transforming the greyest of grey days, like a flower opening into sunshine in a time-lapse film. She was the One. He tried to make sure she knew she was the One, but she already knew. He had hoped he could also be her one, even felt like he was – but only for a while

And so he settled down. But it turned out settling down turned was not what the titles wanted of him. Settling down was just not what they had on their agenda. For a while they just ignored him, but increasingly in recent times, they picked on him. They hounded him. They questioned his every action. It got him down, and it got her down more

With her, the old lines just did not work anymore. *Trust me, I'm a celebrated author*: once she had loved the stories he wove, but she was no longer interested, no longer cared. *Nothing shocks me, I'm a storyteller*: for so long, she had hung on his words, listened like it mattered as he explained the world to her and made her laugh out loud in her amazement. Now there was always something just a little more interesting, more tangible, over his shoulder. *I have a plan*: once she would have laughed and asked *Is it a good plan?* He would have answered *I only said it was a plan*, and she would have giggled, then fallen into his arms and into his bed

Now never again could he tell her these things. Never. Now, as he looked on the most beautiful bored face he could imagine, it seemed to say she had decided, she had made her choice, she had ticked the box labelled *none of the above*. Was there no way back for him?

There was one way. There was maybe one way. There was certainly no other way. It was underhand. It was the way that had worked once before. It was deceitful. But already he was dead in her water. If there was nothing left to spoil, then he would settle for empty trickery, since walking away of his own volition seemed beyond him. He drained his mug, picked it up, carried it the short distance to the sink where he rinsed it quickly under the tap. All the while, he stared at the teabag he had left, drying, at the side of the sink, wondering idly how an old-time fortune-teller might have worked her tricks if confronted with one of those

He stared at this lump of brown just a little too long, it seemed, for, in a moment, the whole kitchen, every corner, every last cranny, was full of the simplest, purest evil. You can tell when that happens: it really is much more obvious than you would credit. Had he been more aware, he would have realised it was ten years since he first had this sensation – since last he had it. Ten years to the day. To the minute. Even to the moment

A rasping voice drew his attention. "Oy! Come on, mate! What's going on 'ere? Making me manifest just because you feel like it, just at the drop of a hat like this, is bad enough. But making me manifest through the medium of a teabag – and a used one at that – well, it's hardly polite is it? Hardly shows concern for my wellbeing. Or respect for my status in the evil scheme of things. You'd better have something good to trade, my lad, or you're going to be so deep in it, you won't have a clue which way is out."

He felt his brain racing. He felt protests welling up from every part of him. But he felt his jaw hang loose and useless. "It *was* English breakfast," was all he managed to say

"I bet it wasn't pyramid-shaped though, was it? Do they still make those? I could at least have made a bit of an entrance through a pyramid. If you hadn't already used it. Anyway, I'm here now, and at least you had the decency to drop the blind so I'm not exposing myself to all that sunlight. What can I do you for?"

He could hardly gaze upon the figure before him. He mumbled, "It's her."

"Her? Her who?"

"Her. You know – her. The One."

Screwing up its face even more, if that were possible for a demon, the figure said, "Oh, her. What's up with her?"

"I'm losing her. She's bored."

"Well it's what happens, isn't it? There's plenty more …"

But he snapped back, "I don't want plenty more, especially not if they're fish. I want her. I want the One."

"But she isn't even all that …"

"Yes she is." He could hardly imagine where he was drawing his courage from to argue with a demon. "So stop saying she isn't. Just sort it out for me if you can. Or banish me to some dark corner of your realm and leave me there if you can't."

"Hey, now – hang on a minute." If demons can be indignant, this one was. "Nobody's saying nothing about 'can't'. 'Can't' is just not a word where I'm from. I just think you've got a lot more options …"

"I keep telling you I have got no options. I just have this one big binary choice. It's either the One or it's zero."

"Ooh, hark at this one. *The one big binary choice – it's either the One or it's the zero.* Very metaphorical."

Scorn was not what he needed right now. "Look – is there anything you can do for me or are you just going to stand there taking the mickey?"

"Of course there's stuff I can do. There's no end to the stuff I can do. It's what I'm known for. The real question is, 'What am I going to get in return?'"

He stared down at his shoes. "But you already have my soul."

"Yes. And you spent that up ages ago. I think you probably owe me already – but don't worry. If you've not got anything else up your sleeve that's tradeable, then I'm going to have to come up with something, aren't I? Well as it happens, you're in luck. I have got a proposition for you. Work with me on this one, do me this one favour, and I'll write off all your debt to date and sort her out for you as well. Does that sound like a deal?"

Could he afford to trust the demon? Could he afford not to? "You knew you were going to do this all along, didn't you? You've just been playing with me."

"Of course I was. I'm a demon, aren't I? That's what demons do. You mortals aren't half naïve sometimes. Now – does this mean we've got a deal?"

"No. No it doesn't. Not till you tell me what it is I've got to do, it doesn't. No."

"Oooh, dearie me. That's sounds very much like you're trying to bargain with me. Lucky for you, I'm in a good mood, so fair enough. This is the craic." Now it is often assumed that demons' faces struggle to show human emotion, but it is generally agreed that they can at least grin, and this one was grinning – fit to bust. "Remember that stunt we pulled on the old president, you and me, way back when we first ... collaborated?"

"Ye-es?"

"Well he was a bit of a push-over, wasn't he? In fact even that's overstating it. No pushing was required. As I remember it, all we had to do was just point him in a general direction and he did the rest for us – all by himself."

"True."

"But this new one – much tougher cookie to crumble. However, I'm pretty sure that with your creative talents and my skills in – what shall we say? – presentation? – we can reel her in as well."

ABOUT THE AUTHOR

Bob Mynors was born in Sheffield, England, in October 1951. He is committed to seeking the abolition of the full stop at the end of the paragraph

"You know when the paragraph has ended: there are no more words left to read till the next one starts. If all the full stops at the end of all the paragraphs ever printed in the world were not there, think how much ink would be saved

"I am just doing my bit."

Printed in Great Britain
by Amazon